Hopes, Dreams and Houses.

Jane C McDermott

ACKNOWLEDGMENTS

I would like to thank a lot of people, so get ready:
Firstly, my family and friends for believing in me and not laughing at me
when I said I was going to write a book.
My wonderful Mum for encouraging me and doing all the checking and
spell checking, and printing and reading etc, so if there are any spelling
mistakes, it's my Mums fault!
Also, my fantastic husband for not minding that I have been spending more
time with my book than him.
Lastly, my two wonderful children, I hope this makes you as proud of me as
I am of both of you.
Love you all
xxx

DEDICATION

This book is dedicated to my Wonderful Dad.

My First Love.

Prologue

Where to start....... July 1985 looks as good a place as any.

Clare (that's me!) was 15, it was the last day of term and I had an exciting summer all planned out. What will this summer bring, what will my life bring? I feel I am on the verge of the start of something quite amazing.

Join me as I head through my teenage years to adulthood. The joys of being a teenager in the 1980's, the loves, losses and laughs I will have, to where I am now. A middle-aged woman in her prime....... Or am I???

Main people in my life. I just thought I would give you a quick rundown of my people and the people that I feel need some introduction, people you will get to know and love as much as I do.

Here goes:

Clare: That's me, funny, gorgeous and modest!

Jane: The Best Friend a girl could have, she is all the above, just not as much as me.

Dave: The boyfriend of the Bestie and not a bad lad but more importantly, the hunk, that is Carl's best mate.

Carl: My GOD, end of.

My Mum: Margo. She is a real snob, you get what you pay for and if something is worth buying, it's worth buying twice! I love her though and wouldn't change her.

Brian: My Dad, funny, lovable and a true gent.

Grandma: Amazing woman, true hero and a real lady. Very ladylike, doesn't swear, although I do keep trying to get her to say the odd bugger!

Marie: Janes Mum, she is lovely and a bit like a second Mum but NEEDS to tone down the make-up.

Mark: Jane's Dad, so easy going and only happy when he is having a fag and a cup of tea.

Lilly: Older, much older sister! She does have her head screwed on and she knows exactly what she wants.

James: Brother in law, lovely guy, very hardworking and adores my sister.

This page has been intentionally left blank.
Please feel free to use it for take away orders, telephone
numbers or just to doodle.

Chapter 1

"Papa don't preach" I woke to the heady tones of Madonna and her plight with her father. I pressed snooze on my alarm and rolled over. It was the last day of term and I had mixed feelings.

Excitement at the thought of nearly seven weeks off school, the thought that, when I went back to school in September I would be in my final year, but the dread that today is the day I had been fearing for months, the last day in my life that I will see HIM. The Adonis, my superman, my hero, the love of my life (if only) the Mel to my Kim, the fish to my chips, the .... you get the picture!

Basically, MY Carl. The dreamy, gorgeous and amazing Carl, the love of my life (yes, I've said that before). The one person who made getting up in a morning a joy, at the prospect of seeing him, ok so usually from afar and usually hidden behind someone else because basically, my Carl didn't know my name, had never even made eye contact, in fact didn't even know I existed!!!! Minor details, I thought.

It all started a few months ago. Jane and I were at school when we noticed, well she noticed, Dave and his "flick hair" you know the long fringe that's quite annoying and makes the owner flick their head every three seconds to try and get it out of their eyes, hence the reason it's called a flick.

Anyway, she noticed him walking passed us at the glass house (basically an added bit of school that was made from class, like a conservatory I suppose but no rattan furniture in sight). He had his bag over his shoulder, a ski jacket on and a scarf wrapped that many times round his neck you couldn't see his mouth. He looked like he was going skiing but not much snow or mountains in Rawdon and certainly not a ski in sight. As he walked passed her she said he gave her "the look" I really couldn't say either way as I was far too busy with the vision at the side of him, that I was later to find out was Carl. You know "My Carl".

Now, he had the same on, I don't mean they were dressed in the same clothes, but he had the ski jacket and the scarf and the bag over his shoulder, but he just had that something else. I don't know what it was, but I wouldn't have minded a piece of it. He had an air about him that was quite sure of himself and confident, but he really was unaware as to how goddam gorgeous he was, which made him even more gorgeous. What with that and his slight acne and scarring. I loved a bit of acne and scarring, you know the pock marks that acne can sometimes leave. I don't know what it is, but I love a man (boy) with a bit of scarring. It adds character, don't you think?

Well, he didn't notice me at all, but I still watched him until he was out of sight.

We decided there and then that we would find out who they were. I say they, but what I mean is Jane had decided that she was going to find out who he was (Dave) and I was going to help. We knew quite a few of the girls in the year above so it wouldn't be difficult.

"Dave Nelson, he lives in Yeadon on the Feather Ways", said Catherine, one of the girls in the year above. She worked in a shop on a weekend near where I lived, and I think her Dad played cricket in the same team as my Dad, so I didn't feel bad asking her, I did kind of know her. More importantly, she also confirmed that he didn't have a girlfriend.

At the bus stop that night I told Jane everything I knew.

"Right, where are your Mum and Dad tonight? Are they going out? Can I come up and we will find out his phone number" pleaded Jane.

They were out all right, some bloody function or other, basically I was making tea for myself again, not that I minded but god it gets boring eating on your own, especially when you must cook the bloody stuff yourself first.

So, 6.30 Jane arrived, looking very flushed, I think she had run all the way.

"Oh hi Margo, are you ok? You look lovely, is it another posh do you are going to?" enquired Jane. She knew exactly what to say to my Mum to get her in a good mood.

"Oh, thank you love" scorned Mother, looking over at me as if to enquire why I hadn't said the same.

"You had better be going, you don't want to be late do you and make sure you get there first, get the best seats and you can have a good look at everyone as they walk in without them knowing" said Jane, knowing it would trigger something in my Mum's head immediately.

"Brian! Brian! Come on we are going to be late" shouted Mum

In came Dad, fastening his tie whilst trying to find his keys and put his shoes on all at the same time. "Stop shouting woman, I'm here" moaned Dad. He gave Jane and I that "God help me look" and followed behind her, like a little lost sheep.

"Right, get your phone book out, let's get his number" said Jane.

We thumbed through the telephone directory (a very large and heavy book that contained everyone in Leeds phone number and address, unless they were ex-directory).

"Got it", screamed Jane and she had!! Oh shit, I knew what that meant now, I was going to have to call him.

It was a stupid promise we made to each other a few years ago that we would always do the telephoning on behalf of the other.

"Oh, shit its ringing, ...Erm, Oh Hello is Dave in please?

Yes, its …. Catherine???!!!!!

Shit shit shit shit, that was his Mum, she's gone to get him" I whispered

"Who the chuff is Catherine?" enquired Jane

"Me, you tit, I'm not giving my real name.

Oh hi Dave, sorry to bother you, you don't know me, but we go to the same school. I was just wondering if you were free on Saturday?" I lied and in my best posh accent, just in case he recognised my voice, not that he knew who I was, but you never know.

"Erm no I'm off to the footy and who is this again?" asked Dave and with that I put the phone down.

"What the hell are you doing!" screamed Jane

"Calm down you tit, you didn't want him to know it was you, did you? so, I had got all the information I needed and therefore no need to carry on the conversation, so I ended the call before he was any the wiser. You my dear Jane and I are going to the footy on Saturday and Dave will be there too" I said in a very pleased with myself attitude.

"You my dear friend are bloody amazing" laughed Jane and with that we clinked our coffee cups.

"I just hope he supports Leeds and not Manchester, or we have a long walk on Saturday!" we rolled about laughing.

The next stage of the mission was to find out exactly what team he did support, and I knew just how to do it.

We have a neighbour the same age as Dave and he is a very keen Leeds United supporter, so I rang him to come straight round. He did because he had a soft spot for me, the feeling was NOT mutual as I felt he was a bit, well....... WET.

"Come in Chris, now, you go to the Leeds matches, don't you? where do you sit or stand? are they playing this weekend, and do you know Dave Nelson?" I asked Chris almost shining a light on him to make him talk.

"Errrrrr wellll, I usually stand in the Kop, it's the best atmosphere, Leeds are playing at home on Saturday and no I don't think I do know a Dave Nelson, I probably will if I see him, do you have a picture?" asked Chris.

What do you think we are, stalkers?! I thought.

"No, we don't but thank you, you can go now" I scoffed and with that I ushered him out of the house. Not nice I know but he is very wet and a bit odd so its ok, he's used to it.

"Result!!! Leeds, Leeds, Leeds, Marching on together!!!! "I sang

So, it was all set. We were going to the match on Saturday and with a bit of luck his fit mate would be with him too, fingers crossed.

Chapter 2

Well the football was quite an experience, luckily Janes Dad was a keen supporter, so he took us, thrilled that at least one of his children had his passion but little did he know the real reason for our sudden love of all things Leeds.

So, he dropped us near Makro on the ring road and we just had to walk up the road.

It's a good job there were plenty of people around adorned with Leeds scarves and hats, so we could follow them as we really had no idea where we were going or what to expect.

Jane, being the gobshite she is, asked one of our fellow supporters how we get into the Kop.

"Follow me love, that's where I am heading" said the Leeds Supporter.

"It's the only place to watch the game, best view, all the chants start there and there's always a fight if you're into that kind of thing" he spat, and he carried on talking absolute shite until we were safely inside.

"Woooooah! It's bigger than it looks on the outside" I said whilst I stood looking round, amazed at the sheer size of the place and the chanting had already started! The atmosphere was fantastic!!! I loved it but couldn't help staring at people, watching them, they not only had chants they had claps too.

Certain noises followed by certain clapping and certain pointing!!! This is going to take some getting used to, I thought.

"Play it cool, don't forget we are seasoned supporters, we have been coming years" said Jane trying to look cool.

So, we joined in the chants and pointing and clapping!!!

We were good and then I spotted Dave, it must have been as I was still looking round busy watching people. He saw me too and gave a sort of wave. So, I gave him the same sort of wave back and turned back to face the court or whatever it's called, PITCH, that's it pitch! I turned back to face the pitch and said to Jane – in a sideways mouth motion.

"Don't look now" famous last words, her head was like a bloody owl, round and round until she spotted him.

"Oh god, don't look now, but he's here behind us" said Jane, same sideways mouth action.

No shit!!! the whistle blew for half time and Dave and his mate came down to where we were stood.

"Alright, don't you two go to Benton? I think I've seen you around? enquired Dave.

"Erm yes we do, but I don't remember seeing you" said a very cool Jane.

"Haaaa, oh ok, well I can go if you like" said Dave a bit perturbed.

"Oh no its fine, you can stop, we could do with a bit of protection" said Jane.

I had to hand it to her she was very good.

So, the second half was spent with Jane and Dave laughing and joking. Then there was me, well, when I said earlier

Dave had a mate with him, well I think he must have been his carer or support worker or something because he was an absolute nut job! I didn't even ask him name.

When everyone was chanting, he was clapping, when they were clapping, he was pointing, and it goes on and on. I think he had had a few knocks to the head and looking at his black eye and bust lip he liked a fight.

Walking back to meet Mark, I could vaguely hear Jane and Dave making plans to meet that night. My job here is done and a Saturday night on my own beckons.

No sign of Carl with him and I later found out he doesn't really watch football, so on my part, it was a total waste of time.

Chapter 3

So back to where we were, I was getting ready to make that last ever, first impression.

"Jesus Clare, has your coconut perfume leaked in your bag again" scoffed Jane. As I got to the bus stop.

Just what I needed, my best mate basically telling the whole of the bus stop, that yet again I had applied far too much of my favourite Bodyshop Coconut Oil perfume. Well, I put more on, when I am nervous.

"Shut up div, I just slipped as I put it on" I said, to which Jane gave me a knowing look!

The bus approached, and we went straight upstairs for the journey to school. Upstairs was the only place to be, it meant we could have the first one of our cigs for the day.

We bought 10 between us every day, 50p each out of our dinner money. One on the bus to school, one at break, two at lunchtime (well it was an hour) then the last on the bus home.

We chatted all the way, without pausing for breath, about what we were going to do this summer. We had a holiday planned in the middle and had just started going to the pub, so it would be a good summer. Well it would be better if we were allowed into town, but we weren't, both parents had allowed us to go locally but town was out of bounds.

Old Ball at Horsforth it was then as far as they were concerned.

Benton Park Grammar School, we had arrived! We jumped off and ran over the road (obviously taking note of Tufty and the Green Cross Code).

The group of girls waiting were all waving excitedly at us, they made up the rest of our little clique.

We were now linking arms and laughing as we approached.

The noise of the girls grew louder, as we squealed with delight at the topic of what we were all going to do in the holidays and carried on all the way to our classroom.

I couldn't help but look over the field, where Carl would walk in a morning to get to school and back again at night, just to check if he was there or not.

He wasn't!

The morning dragged, none of the teachers really wanted to be there and neither did any of the pupils. Finally, at last, the bell rang for break. We were up and out of our seats faster than a fast thing, on fast island.

Jane was too caught up with Andy, (one of our mates) talking about Neighbours, to notice that I had inadvertently taken them on a slight detour, via the 5th form common room, on the way to the ginnel, for our 2nd cig of the day.

Pray tell why would I do such a thing???? I needed the extra steps for my Fitbit (yes, I know it's not been invented yet, humour me) I WANTED A SNEAKY GLIMPSE OF CARL DUUUUUUR!

He was there! Oh, my shitting god, shit, shit, shit, he was there!!! Looking all gorgeous and WELL FIT!!! Play it cool Clare, come on girl get it together!

Noooooo, I was so busy trying to look, but trying to make it look like I wasn't looking that the inevitable happened, you guessed it, straight into the bin! Well not into the bin, as inside it, but straight into the side, with enough force to make the whole of the common room stop what they were doing and stare!!! Nay, not just the common room, the WHOLE FUCKING SCHOOL!!! Nay the WHOLE FUCKING WORLD! Well it certainly felt like it, but I would swear down that he saw me, he noticed me and gave me a little smile! He did, honest to god he did. Ok so it might have been a laugh, but he had seen me and smiled, well I was going with that.

"Haaaaaaaaaaaaaaa what a spaz, what the hell are you doing you tit and why are we here" said Jane quite confused now as to where we were.

You see, although me and Jane were the best of friends, I had never really mentioned my lust for Carl, it was difficult because Carl was only bloody Dave's best mate and Dave was Janes boyfriend!!!! I know, I know, it would be perfect, double dating, best man and bridesmaids at weddings god mother and father for each other but I just couldn't bring myself to tell her because I knew, without a shadow of a doubt, that Jane would tell Dave and I would DIE if she did, so I had decided not to tell her, as hard as it was, especially after 2 halves of lager when the beer gob started!!! (I was 15 and it would take a while for me to hold my own, on the drink front!)

"Oh sorry, I don't know I wasn't thinking, my heads all over the place with my Grandad" I said. It wasn't a total lie, I was worried about my Grandad, who was in hospital losing his battle with cancer (said in a hushed whispered tone as we do when we say that word).

The three of us carried on and I couldn't help but look over my shoulder, back at the common room and he was stood staring at me, grinning!!

Happy Happy Happy. Ok so he didn't admit his dying love, but it was a start and for the last 6 months, this is the most interest he has shown, so I am taking it!!! Hell Yes!!

Well, what with worrying about my Grandad (and I was) and the thoughts of what had happened earlier, before I knew it, the final bell had gone!!!

SCHOOL WAS OUT FOR SUMMER and that meant only one thing – grab Jane as fast as I could and run to the field to bump into Dave (and Carl obvs) so that Jane could make plans with Dave for that evening (no mobile phones in these black and white days, we had to TALK directly to the person and ring their home and spend 5 hours talking to their deranged Grandma before we got to talk to our beaus (god where did that word come from ? Ye Olde Englishy)!

They were there, just in front, as they always were.

"Dave" shouted Jane.

"Hey" cool as ever was our Dave and Carl just did his usual "Alright"

"So, about tonight" …and off she went as they walked over the field, leaving me and Carl, kind of walking together and kind of not, but close enough for me to smell his beautiful smell of Kouros! God, I loved that smell, so much so, I asked for a bottle at Christmas, much to my Mum's confusion "It's fashion Mum to wear aftershave" yes right! It just reminded me of Carl. She did believe me though, as I did wear Pringle golf jumpers and Farrar trousers! Hey, I was a dresser and proud of it!

Any who, (that's any how if you weren't sure and not dead cool like us) before I knew it we had got to the fence which meant only one thing, he would be gone, forever.

"See ya around" said Carl as he winked (yes, an actual sexy wink, to me).

I don't know how long I was stood there but the sound of Jane shouting "Come on you tit, you are gonna miss the bus" was enough to see me running over the road to get on the bus just before it left.

"What was all that about with you and Carl?" Enquired Jane with a grin "He fancies you, Dave says he's been asking about you".

OH MY FUCKING FUCKING GOD, ARE YOU KIDDING ME!

Play it cool, for fucks sake play it cool and don't start blushing or sweating, play it down, you can do this, come on, you've got it, I thought to myself.

"Eh? who's Carl? I said. All the time feeling myself getting redder and redder. Play it cool Clare, you can do this, no one suspects a thing (I said to myself again and obviously not out loud as that would be ridiculous, even for me).

I think I got away with it, as it wasn't mentioned again, Jane was too busy trying to dig the last two fags out of her bag and find some matches for the journey.

As we got off the bus, Jane and I decided on our plans for that night, we were meeting at the Leeds United Supporters Club, at the Cricket Club, in Horsforth, near the Old Ball.

We started going to the matches firstly, so that Jane could watch Dave (before they became an item) and so that I could ogle Mervin Days bum as he bent at his goal and Ian Snodding and his gorgeous tash and locks.

Seven o' clock it was and with that we parted and went our own way.

I couldn't stop thinking about what Jane had said! Maybe it was true, but I doubted it as he hadn't said anything to me and it's not as if he could send a friend request on Facebook or like my posts on Instagram now was it.

Chapter 4

Tonight, the meeting seemed to go on and on and I really wasn't in the mood, you see, when I had got home from school I was surprised to see someone was home. Panicking when I saw my Mum's car, I ran into the house (my Mum usually worked till 5 and wasn't home till after half past) to see my poor little Grandma looking all lost and trying her best to seem cheery, in front of me.

"What's happened? Is Grandad Ok?" I said, panic rising at the thought of what the answer was going to be.

"He's not good love, the doctors have just had me and your Grandma in to say they will be doing some more tests tonight, but it doesn't look good I'm afraid, so Grandma is stopping with us tonight, so we can set off to the hospital first thing in the morning" said my Mum.

I ran over to my Grandma and gave her a massive hug that was greatly reciprocated, and we sat together like that for ages, we were very close, and I adored my Grandma, the feeling was mutual.

"So, what have you got planned now that you have broken up" said Grandma trying desperately to keep things normal.

"Supporters club tonight, but I'll give it a miss and stay in with you two" I said.

"I don't think so Lady" said Grandma, "You need to get out and do fun things and carry on as normal, your Grandad would want you to"

With that and a quick kiss on my Grandmas cheek I ran up to my bedroom to start getting ready although I really couldn't be bothered but I did as you know, I mentioned it a few paragraphs up.

So, the meeting was at a close and Jane had the strangest look on her face, one that you weren't quite sure what she was up to, the look that filled you with dread as to what exactly she had planned.

"What" "what are you looking like that for? You look like you've had a stroke" I said to Jane, to which we both cackled and said at the same time "I should be so lucky".

We were still laughing, as we walked down the drive of the cricket club.

"You are stopping at mine tonight still, you know, what with your Grandad?" said Jane with concern.

"Why is he coming too" I laughed and then carried on "Yes, my Grandma said I have to carry on, so I might as well"

"He will be ok you know, I can feel it in my water" said Jane.

That was one of our favourite sayings in times of need.

As we reached the gate at the bottom of the drive I was sure I could see Dave at the bus stop. Oh, great I thought, I'm stopping at Janes and will be playing gooseberry all night, at least till he goes home and it's not as if Marie (Janes Mum) is in tonight, it's her Calorie Counter club in the park.

Jane at this point had that stupid look on her face again and it wasn't until I looked over at the bus stop again that I realised what she was laughing at.

"Alright"

Fuck! Am I seeing things??? Carl, here, near where I live and presumably to see me or am I grasping at straws I thought.

Jane and Dave were a bit in front by now, so we both started to walk behind.

"I don't know if Jane has said anything, but I've been asking Dave to find out if you are seeing anyone. I've seen you around school but didn't have the courage to come talk to you, so I thought if I leave it till I have left school and if you say no, I don't have to bump into you" said Carl. All the time looking down, he really was so sweet and really quite shy in a funny sort of way

"Say no to what? that was the first thing I said

"To going out with me?" replied Carl, still looking a bit sheepish, god love him.

"Oh Right, I didn't even think you knew I existed" I said

By now my mind in a whirl and not quite sure what was happening.

As we walked and talked we got to the park and noticed Jane and Dave were sat on the wall, we joined them.

"Soooooooooooooo are you two an item or what?" said Dave.

"Erm, yes I guess so" I said, with the biggest beam on my face!

Looks like this summer is going to be pretty good! I had bagged the man of my dreams, literally.

As it turns out Carl had noticed me, every time that Jane had met up with Dave, but he didn't have the nerve to talk to me, apparently, I give off an air of assured self-confidence and great popularity, something I was unaware of and that made it hard for Carl to talk to me for fear of rejection. He came across as the cool kid, the one everyone fancied but he was very deep and oh such an amazing snog!

This was the start of something amazing, everything I could have dreamt of and it kept me and Jane up all-night planning what the four of us were going to do together and what things we could get up to. I was in a daze all night. I really couldn't believe my luck and we were so thrilled and talked and planned and laughed and danced about and laughed a bit more but all that was about to come crashing down before I knew it.

Chapter 5

Me and Carl were at the top of a Mountain, the sun was shining, and the birds were tweeting, and I don't mean informing their followers of what they had eaten for tea.

We were laughing and smiling at each other, this was just perfect but then a phone started to ring? Where is that coming from? This doesn't seem right - there it goes again - the persistent trill of a house phone (I say house phone, it could only really be a house phone or a pay phone, nothing else had been invented).

We both looked confused, trying to work out where it was coming from when I suddenly felt my body shake – I awoke, startled to find Jane's Mum, Marie, waking me to say that my Mum was on the phone.

I ran down to the phone, picking it up, shaking, knowing that whoever needed to talk to me now, at this time in the morning, wasn't going to be telling me I had won Miss Leeds.

"Hello" I said, really not wanting to hear what was going to be said – it can' t be bad news about my Grandad, surely they wouldn't have his test results back yet??

"Hi love, Its Mum, I just thought I had better let you know that the hospital has just called, it's worse than we thought. They don't think your Grandad will last the day and they have asked that me and your Grandma go down straight away. Your Dad is going to take us, but I knew you would want to know."

I was speechless, I really didn't expect that at all, what should I do, what could I do? I didn't want to leave my Mum talking too long for fear of missing him and him being on his own. Worst case, I thought he might not be coming out, but I hoped that he would have had longer left than a few hours!!! Oh god, why him, why now?? Just as things are going amazing this happens. It's like someone is punishing me for daring to be happy!

"Do you want me to come with you? I can meet you there?" I said secretly hoping my Mum said no. I obviously wanted to see my Grandad but really wasn't wanting to rush down to watch him die.

"No, not unless you really want to but I think it would be best for you to stay with Jane and Marie, I've told Marie, and she said she was going to take you both out for lunch, try keep things normal, your Grandma will really need us now love, she is devastated, as we all are but all those years together, she is going to find it really hard" said my Mum with a deep sigh.

"OK well, tell Dad to ring if he hears anything and I'll come back home once he's back, unless he is staying with you?" I said

"He is going to play it by ear. We will let you know love if anything happens" said Mum, now her voice fading as she is clearly realising the seriousness of the situation in hand.

"OK Mum I love you and tell Grandma I love her too, ooh and Dad and...."

I paused, tell Grandad I love him and always will and tell him I will make him proud and I will look after you and

Grandma" with that I fell to pieces and couldn't stop my tears. I was sobbing uncontrollably when Marie came in and put her arm around me, took the phone off me and told Margo not to worry about me and that she will look after me and to take care, she was thinking about them all and the usual "if there is anything I can do, just let me know" garbage that people say when they don't know what to say but feel they have to say something in order to stop it being so awkward .

With that Marie replaced the receiver and gave me the biggest and tightest hug anyone could.

"Now come on, let's go get ready and go out to Ilkley for lunch, your Grandad loves Ilkley and we can go up on the moor and have a little think" said Marie trying to do her best Mum of the year bit.

Why do people think we need to think, what would I think about, the fact that I will never see my Grandad again? That my Grandma will be devastated and my Mum and me come to think of it will be?? Oh yes great one that Marie, let's go up on Ilkley Moor and THINK! Fuck off I really can't be arsed be with you and your fucking thinking, go screw yourself Marie and stick your lunch right up your arse. But obviously I didn't say that, I smiled politely and went to get a shower.

Lunch was ok and yes Marie made us go up to the top of Ilkley Moor and think!!! By this time, Jane and I were both hysterically laughing – Marie thought it was grief. It was kind of, but it was more the look on Marie's face all morning, you know that sad pathetic "you are grieving, and

I am here for you chick" look! Yada Yadda and all that shiz.

By the time we got back to their house I noticed my Dad's car. That can only mean one thing. We walked through the door to find my Dad and Mark (Janes Dad) having a cup of tea. As soon as we walked in my Dad got to his feet, walked over to me and hugged me and gave me the "arm stroke", that he is so famous for. Good News or sad news, my Dad did the "arm stroke" to tell you he loved you and was there for you but not sure what else to do.

"I'm so sorry love, he's gone, it was very peaceful, and we were all there with him" said Dad

Gone? Gone where? Why do people say that, why don't they just say he is dead, it's not like I didn't know he was dying. By saying he's gone I picture him with a suitcase walking up the stairs to heaven, to be greeted by everyone that has "gone" before him.

Actually, that gave me great comfort, so I will give Brian that one! Well done Bri I don't feel that bad now.

It had been decided between my Dad and Mark that it might be best if I stopped with them again, just for tonight, so they could concentrate on Grandma and Dad had brought me some clean clothes. Steady on Bri, I thought, I am only staying the night not a fortnight, as I saw the C&A bag bulging with a mixture of mine and my Mum's clothes, he really didn't get the fact that me and my Mum had our own clothes!

So as the days and weeks passed I did all I could to help my Grandma with her grief. We had a wonderful service in memory of my Grandad, all his favourite Hymns, favourite flowers and favourite food at the doo afterwards. Jane was there for support and so was Marie and Mark as a mark of respect, which was nice.

I was still totally infatuated with Carl and I am very pleased to say, I think he was with me. If we didn't see each other every other day we would spend hours talking on the phone. Much to my Dad's frustration as he was sick of "no one ever talks in this house to each other there is always someone on that bloody phone, well I will show you all, I've put a phone lock on"!

What he hadn't thought about is that he only put one on the phone downstairs and forgot the one in his and Mum's bedroom!!! Hee Hee!! Let's see you work that one out when you get the bill!

Carl was at college most days and when he wasn't there he was working on a building site, labouring but being taught a few things too. I am not 100% sure what his course was at college, but it was something to do with architecture and designing buildings. All I know is that if he passed this he could go onto University. If it was Leeds or near I wasn't bothered, and I was so proud of him.

It got to the time to go on holiday with Jane. What a bloody laugh – Italy on a coach – it only took nearly two days and the coach was driven by a right perv. Jane and I managed to bagsy the two front seats (one each) so we could lie down a bit and apply our special ointment bought at Boots that guaranteed an amazing tan if you put it on all over your body for 3 days before you went out in the sun, thinking about it now I have no idea what it was meant to do but it was pretty difficult trying to apply it without Peter Perv watching whilst he should have been watching the bloody road !

Lido de Jesolo! Italy at its finest !!! haaaaa! It was wall to wall bars but shitting hell it was dear! No 50p for half a lager there I can tell you, so we opted to go to the local supermarket and have a few before we went out and smuggle the rest into whichever club took our fancy that night.

The holiday went by in a whirl – before we knew it Peter Perv was picking us up again for the shitty two-day journey home.

As we got off in Leeds my Dad was there to meet us and to give Jane a lift home.

I couldn't wait to get home to see my Mum and ring Carl. As soon I heard his voice and he heard mine and he knew I was home he told me "get the kettle on I will be over in 5" what a cutey and he was – over in 5 as well as cute!

The weeks passed, and we became inseparable, we had been going out with Jane and Dave on a Saturday, but Jane and I had been having our Friday nights in TOWN!!!! Yeah, we were going to town. The parents didn't know obviously but we had dared to go. The Bank was the place to be, a cool bar with cool people and the bouncers really couldn't give a shit if you were 18 or not "you 18" they would ask occasionally – "erm yes course we are" we would reply in our best 18-year-old voices and off we went, allowed to go in. It was quite a dark bar, but we would get positioned at the far end of the bar and sit and chat and watch all the people as they passed us to go to the loo. Sometimes others from school would be in but if not, we got talking to other people in there. It was our girly time, we loved the boys, but we needed girly time, after all we were strong and very independent women!

Saturdays usually consisted of all of us at mine or Jane's, depending whose parents were out and sometimes at the local, the Abbey. We could get in there and have a couple of beers. We knew the landlord and he was happy with us being there "as long as there is no swearing, spitting or necking you can come in" were the famous words of the landlord every time we went in.

Things were going well, no, they were fucking amazing, but I wasn't counting my chickens, I was sure if I was gloating about being so happy or just by being so happy something terrible would happen. Well I was a paranoid teenager, what do you expect.

Time was going so fast, here we were again back at school.

I didn't have the same urge to get up in a morning, I didn't need it, I had my man and sometimes he even picked me up from school. He had done so well with his driving lessons and passed first time and his Mum and Dad were so thrilled, they bought him a car!!!

Now we didn't have to wait till the parents went out for some "alone time" we could have it whenever we wanted, just me, Carl and Daisy the car.

It opened so much more to do, not only was it our own little passion wagon but Sundays saw the four of us being able to travel further afield than the Abbey to The Sun Inn and to this day I have no idea where it is, it just seemed to appear in the middle of nowhere and anyone that was anyone would go. It wasn't even about going for a drink it was more to be seen!

Not only had Carl passed his driving test he was now well on the way to passing his college course which would enable him to go to University.

Not to tempt fate but again things were good.

The final school year for Jane and I were the best, we were the oldest in the school, apart from the 6th formers, but they didn't count.

We got more freedom and we were able to work on a weekend. I decided on hairdressing, well I say I decided, it was kind of decided for me as my sister was a hairdresser and they needed a Saturday girl and well I got the job. I loved it and I don't know why I didn't stick at it when I left school, it's funny how things turn out.

The day I went on stand down after my exams I pictured having the rest of May and the whole of the summer to decide what I was going to do with my life, oh how wrong I was.

Mum & Dad treated us to tea out, the Outside Inn, near where we lived. We all went, me, Carl, Mum, Dad, Grandma, my sister and James all to celebrate me finishing my exams. Full and content heading home, Carl and I started talking about living together. Obviously, it wouldn't be for ages, he didn't earn much at the builders and would have to do less hours when he went to Uni, but we could dream. We even started looking through my Mum's catalogues to pick furniture.

As we got home I had just been nominated by the family to make "a nice cup of tea" when the phone rang. I could hear my Dad getting very excited and just keep saying "bloody real" which along with the arm rub was another of his little quirks.

"Who was that love?" asked Mum when he eventually came off the phone.

"Our Barbara, she's only gone and got our Clare an interview where she works, for an office junior, I think it's pretty much in the bag, but they have to go through the motions" and with that he paused and then "Bloody Real"

Erm hello father I am here, and I can decide if I want to go for this job can't I or has it just been decided??? It was the latter as I later found out.

So, there I was 16 and in full time work. It was ok actually, some nice people and quite a few younger ones, not quite as young as 16 but I was very mature for my age.

Chapter 6

Time went by and being a grown up made you realise just how quickly time flies and before I knew it I had been in full time employment for over a year.

So, I am working and doing ok, I am no longer the office junior, but I am now a trainee Motor Insurance Handler and we have taken on a new office junior, god was I that immature and giddy when I was that age! Ok so there's only about 18 months in us but that's a lot when you are 17 and a half.

We have spent quite a lot of time recently at work discussing my 18th Birthday Party, it's a must and the party of the year in our group.

Ok so maybe not the party of the year but it was to be held at the local Civic Hall, my uncle that wasn't really my uncle, but my Dad's best friend, was going to do the disco for me, but he had to back out as he had previously been diagnosed with a brain tumour and was just getting over his operation, so another of my Dad's friends, not an uncle though, was to take over.

The food was sorted, Mum had got some caterers she knew to do it, she loved that it was caterers and not her and kept inadvertently telling people "Her" caterers were doing the buffet, it was ok , nothing special just the usual sandwiches, sausage rolls, pork pies, a bit of quiche, few crisps and nuts and just to be a bit swanky, and that little bit better than Jessie down the street whose daughter had just had an 18th , Pate, olives and garlic bread !!! It was 1989 – my mother was just like Mrs Bucket, only yet again we didn't know that because that character hadn't been brought to life yet.

Carl was there, obviously, Jane and Dave, Marie and Mark, Carl's Mum and Dad and sisters and all my lot. Aunties that were real aunties, aunties that were just my Mum's best friends, uncles, sister and her husband, few neighbours that were neighbours, not aunties or uncles or even friends, just neighbours but well, there was Olives and Pate and Garlic bread, of course the neighbours were invited!

I'm guessing by now you are getting the picture of my Mum, love her to bits but when she started with her fancy ways my Dad would just say "Yes Dear"! as he rolled his eyes and knew this was going to cost him.

One of the best things my Mum ever did was the day I had been to a friend's house for tea (or supper as they called it) when I was about 10, her Mum and Dad must have been quite old when they had her because the first time my Mum saw them at School she thought they were my friends Grandparents – that didn't go down well, anyway I was at her house and I knew they were posh because they had top and bottom towels each, one for the top half of their body and one for their bottom ????!!!! So here I am, at their house, ready for tea oops I mean supper when Mrs Carlton asked me if I liked Caviar – well I was a little confused and thought she meant pate, why I don't know but I did and so I said yes, my Mum gets it from that deli every week.

Oh, the look on her face was nearly as good as when Mr Jones from three doors down asked my Mum if she rented her washing machine!!! What do you think Mr Jones, the lady of the house does not rent, she owns!!! Well via

Grattan and their very good buy now and pay 25p a week for the next 234 years terms that they offered.

"Each Week" said Mrs Carlton through pursed lips "Oh how nice"

It wasn't until she passed me two teeny tiny crackers with balls on I knew I had made a right balls up!!! But being the daughter of the lady of the house I ate it, gipping with every mouthful at the horrible fishy balls I had in my mouth – I could make some smutty comment there, but I was only 10 and it would seem very inappropriate.

So, after supper I thanked them for tea, quickly correcting myself to supper and bid my farewell to my friend and headed home to tell my Mum what we had had for supper,

"So, what did Mrs Carlton make you for tea" Enquired my Mum the second I walked through the door.

"Oh, it wasn't tea Mummy, it was supper" first mistake, the hackles on the back of her neck were up, I could tell, she had that look in her eye.

"Silly me of course it was supper, and what did you have for SUPPER" really emphasising the word SUPPER.

"Caviar" I said, because we did. I didn't think anything of it until I saw the look on my Dad's face, the roll of his eyes which meant "This was going to cost him yes we would be having caviar from on.

"C A V I A R "now even more emphasised!! I swear I could see steam coming out of her ears in a cartoon like fashion and the only thing that really made her day was when I explained that silly me had got confused and told

Mrs Carlton that we had it every week, I have never seen my Mum laugh so much, Mrs Carlton Nil points Mother aka Lady of the House 2 points. Game set and match to Mum.

So, you can gather from that, bless her she always did and still does like the finer things in life even if she tells a few odd little stretches of the truth to ensure people know just how grand she really is.

Back to the party, it was a great success, I got so many Keys with 18 on and I thought you only got them at 21??? A nightie that went down to my ankles??!! A gold gate bracelet , earrings, some towels for my bottom drawer because one of my aunties that wasn't my auntie worked in promotions and I'm guessing they didn't sell that well, money, a swatch watch from Carl that was so cool the numbers were all over the place and the hands were really weird but this is the 80's it is very trendy and a Yellow, grey and white diamond Pringle Jumper from my Dad as a little joke gift so he could have his back .

All in all, it was a great success and now that I was an adult my Mum and Dad decided that Carl could stop over at our house in my room!!!! Whoop! Whoop!! RESULT!!!

I love being 18.

Chapter 7

Sticking to the theme of being an adult Mum decided that now I was a grownup, we should do grown up things together, so she decided one Tuesday evening that we should walk up to Stuarts Wine bar and share a bottle of wine and have a good chat. So, we did. Mum ordered a bottle of wine from the menu with an air about her that she know what she was talking about.

We sat drinking it and Mum dropped the bombshell" When do you think you will be moving out" Jesus Margo, I have just turned 18, is there a time limit?

"It's just that me and your Dad were talking, now that your sister has left, and you are in a serious relationship we were thinking of selling up and downsizing" said Mum.

"What! no way please Mum don't do that" I screeched

"I always pictured that I would bring my children to my old house to see you, it's my home, where I grew up and where all my memories were made"

As I sat there, it just felt empty and I wanted to go straight over to see Carl to see what he thought, am I being silly and over reacting?

No, I am not!

I don't want them to move, in fact I don't want to move, I'm not ready for the big wide world yet, however much I adore and love Carl, I really can't see that happening anytime soon.

The tone of the night went downhill rapidly after that, I couldn't get it out of my mind and I could have cried when we eventually got home. I say hi to my Dad and go straight upstairs. I went into my Mum and Dad's bedroom and dialled Carl's number.

He answered, "You won't believe what my Mum and Dad are doing, they are selling the house and moving away, I don't know what I am going to do, where am I going to live"? I had no sooner got the last word out when Carl said "get the kettle on I'm on my way"

I instantly felt much better, protected and cared for and knew that he would sort it out. No more than 10 minutes passed, and I heard the front door go, his familiar voice greeting my Mum and Dad. I pulled myself together and waited for him to come upstairs to me as I was now sat in my bedroom waiting for him.

No sign, no footsteps, nothing. Just faint voices coming from downstairs. I left it as long as I could and then my patience ran out and I reluctantly went downstairs.

"Oh, here she is, drama queen" scoffed my Dad

What the hell, what was he on about? Drama queen make that homeless drama queen if you don't mind, I thought.

"Now what have you been telling Carl, that we sold the house and you are out on the street" said Dad to which all three of them laughed.

"Erm well yes, that's what Mum said" I said quite venomously, I wasn't going to be laughed at, I was homeless. Oh god, I was going to end up like the little match girl, I thought, all dirty in grey clothes selling all sorts of things just to buy some chestnuts???!!! That thought made me question my sanity – I know I am a bit of a drama queen at the best of times, but this was way too far, even for me. I snapped out of it and sat down, waiting for an explanation.

"Your Mum and I have simply been weighing up the possibilities of maybe downsizing, we don't need a big house now and we thought with the money we have left after we have bought something a bit smaller it will help you and your sister out. She has a baby on the way and could do with a bit of extra cash and you and Carl, I am assuming, will be looking at buying your own place in the next couple of years.

It's a decision we will make as a family Clare, you won't come back from work one day and find all your belongings in the garden, you are silly sometimes and you had Carl rushing over straight away on a bit of whim really" laughed my Dad." Come here, you are a daft little thing you know, pulling me onto his knee (never too old for that) but I do love you" said Dad, laughing again and to show how much he loved me he did "the arm stroke" say no more.

After the conversation we went through every possibility and my parents decided they would look to see what slightly smaller houses were available, but in the same area and I made them promise that!!! I wouldn't be able to afford to live round here for a while, so they had to! They just did, end of.

It got Carl and I talking more and more about houses and what happened over the next few months made our mind up for us.

Carl called me one night to say he couldn't come over that night, he sounded weird and didn't want to stay and chat, he made that obvious, so we said our goodbyes and I went to feel sorry for myself in my bedroom, in the dark. I must have fallen asleep as my Mum woke me up to come downstairs. She looked a bit odd and just motioned for me to follow her. My heart sank when I walked into the living room. Carl's Mum was sat there looking very upset. "Hi love, don't worry Carl is ok, but I would sit down if I was you"

The long and short of it was that Carl's biological Dad had left the family when Carl was about 8 months old, so the guy he called Dad, wasn't really his Dad but he was his Dad because he had brought him up.

Any who, his biological Dad had been killed in a car accident and Carl's Mum had found out earlier in the day and then only because a solicitor had called her.

The solicitor explained that after the accident the lady who was in the car with "sperm donor" was his girlfriend and she had arranged all his funeral etc but couldn't get in touch with any family because she didn't know where to start. She knew where he had come from and what Carl's Mum was called but had to get a solicitor to track them down because the Estate needed settling and old spermio had left it to his children and quite a hefty sum it was too.

She went on to explain that even though she had always been very open with Carl about spermio and his Dad (that's his step Dad but he calls Dad) Carl had taken it quite bad and taken himself out for a drive. By this time, I felt dreadful, he was always there for me, but I couldn't help him with this one as no one knew where he was. His Mum had thought he might have come here?? Well as we were talking he did turn up, he had been home, and his Dad had told him how worried his Mum was and that she was at ours, so he came straight over. It was the first time I had seen him cry and god did he cry, it made me love him more. He sat hugging his Mum, both in tears, it was heart breaking. We all left them to it and went into the kitchen to make the "this will make you feel better cup of tea".

We briefly, in very hushed tones, discussed how horrendous it all was and how we thought we would we deal with it. Carl doesn't remember his Dad / spermio (seems disrespectful to call him that now he is dead, but he did leave them) but it must still hurt and like his Mum said they did love each other and had all their three children whilst they were in love, so it must be hard for her too.

They called us back in and Carl was more in control and said he felt much better for talking to his Mum and that he had just got up and left when he found out as he needed to process the whole situation by himself before he spoke to anyone about it.

He stayed that night and we talked and talked until we fell asleep in each other's arms, the only way to sleep in my eyes.

Chapter 8

A couple of weeks after all this happened, Carl came around and showed me the cheque he had been sent from the solicitor. Well I actually felt like throwing myself back on my bed and throwing the cheque up in the air in the style of movie stars on films when they throw the cash up in the air but I decided against it a) it was a cheque and would just look a bit shit and b) it was money from his dead Dad /sperm donor RIP even though I feel you were a bit of a tit for leaving but hey I don't know the circumstances and therefore don't feel I can judge so maybe a semi tit but still RIP - he is still dead !

"I was thinking, my course is going really well, and I am going back on the building site in a few weeks so if they like what they see, my boss has said they will pay my Uni fees. I will have to transfer to another course, it will take longer but it will mean I won't have any Uni fees to fund and I will be getting a regular wage whilst I work and what with that and the money I was left (he never says money my Dad left or even sperm donor as that's just my secret sick name, he always refers to it as just money he was left) we should really start looking for a place to buy together, your wage has gone up and I think we could borrow about £35,000 and there are some lovely one bedroom flats in Farsley that would be ideal, half way between your parents and mine and cheap to maintain. What do you think?" said Carl.

What do I think, I have redecorated every room in this new place and hung pictures on the wall by the time it has taken you to get that out is what I am thinking but out loud I just squealed, threw my arms round him and then ran downstairs to tell my Mum and Dad?

"I'm moving out, Carl and I are buying a one bedroom flat in Farsley" I shouted running into the living room.

"Eh, oh Right" said Dad looking very confused and Mum just squealed with me, very excited at the prospect of her now moving onto stage 2 of let's get this house sold and get one of the new builds in the village that will make me look more fabulous than I do now, at the cricket club.

Over the next few weeks we viewed so many properties that when we finally got the keys, I wasn't sure which we had bought but it was as we had initially thought, a nice one bed apartment (not a flat, I am my mother's daughter) in Farsley. It was perfect, we moved our very few belongings in, mainly a kettle and toaster, a few mugs and a quilt – they weren't called duvets then I don't think.

Everyone we knew rallied round and before we knew it we had everything we could ever have wanted. Nothing matched, and most things were things people pretended they were giving us because they loved us but some of them were an excuse for them to dump them on us and save them a trip to the tip.

We decided to decorate the living room, living room the only room that is not a bathroom, bedroom or kitchen. We had four rooms in total, but we loved it.

We set about getting rid of the dreadful woodchip wallpaper that people in the 80's thought was great. It was no blown vinyl and a poor man's artex. It was basically piss poor, thin paper with shavings of wood stuck to the inside so when you finally got the shit paper off you were left with scraping thousands of tiny bits of wood off the wall. Then we tackled the ceilings, getting rid of the major fire hazard that was polystyrene ceiling tiles. They too were a bastard to get off as they broke into millions of teeny tiny pieces, stuck to your hair and your shell suit (ask your Mum or nan if you don't have any idea what they were, basically a highly flammable silky, no need to iron, leisure suit frequented by people, like me who thought they looked amazing in them on a weekend but only in the house) They were horrendous, but a fashion must!

So, all this finally completed we decided on fitting a false Dado rail not to be confused with a dildo as my Mum did! For all her fine upbringing and need for the finer things in life she had a dreadful habit of using the wrong word when she was trying to impress. I don't think she impressed her neighbour, the one whose daughter had her 18th with the "caterers" just before me, remember?! When she boasted "Jane and Carl are decorating their apartment, they are getting lovely wallpaper, striped at the bottom and flowers at the top and separated with a dildo rail! I honestly thought I would die laughing when she told us but soon stopped as Carl pointed out "I'm impressed that she has heard of a dildo yet a little worried"

Jesus H!!! The thought of my Mum and Dad and toys and sex and oh for fucks sake, stop it now, a little bit of sick just came into my mouth. THEY ARE MY PARENTS and THEY ARE OLD!!! They Must be 50 - They don't have sex or kiss or use toys!! They just don't, now change the topic!

So, we had our Dado rail fitted and our striped and flowered wallpaper and a border – forget the less is more this is the 90's, time of acid and potpourri and shell suits, lacy net café curtains (just at the bottom half of your window to give that continental feel) and silky heavy curtains with swags and tails and bits at the top and tie backs and all that shite. Less is more- I DON'T THINK SO!

The only thing we couldn't afford in the "room" was a new fire -it was a Cannon gas fire, stuck on the wall with no fire place, just the fire on the wall with no style what so ever but a lovely place to put your cup of coffee and the carpet, the previous owners must have been on bloody acid, it was hideous, though, thinking about it, I strongly doubt it as she was 80 if she was a day and I think they had carried him out in a box three year previously. Still it was horrendous, shitty brown with the biggest and brightest flowers anyone has ever seen.

A cheeky little rug should sort that out and I know the perfect one to get.

You know how I said earlier, about my Mum, and her need for the finer things in life and to be just that little bit better than the Jones's, well I was going to put her to the test.

Carl and I called round one Saturday afternoon. Dad was at cricket, so I knew we had Mum to ourselves.

"Hi Mum, only us" I shouted as I let myself in and through to the kitchen.

We sat chatting, Mum made us have something to eat because we obviously were living off takeaways and not very good food. Au Contraire, mother dear, luckily for me Carl was quite a whiz in the kitchen, but I wasn't going to tell her she might stop feeding us.

Any who – there I go again! We sat chatting when I brought up that I had bumped into Pamela (the one who had the party and the caterers blah blah blah) well she had been saying she was looking for a rug and she had come across one in Asda, as they do home furnishings now, and as soon as she saw it she thought of yours in your living room. She said how much she had always loved that rug when she used to come around to play so she didn't hesitate, and she bought it.

"Asda, she said my rug was NOT from Asda" spat my Mum

"No, she just said she had got one that was like your rug in Asda, it wouldn't be the same quality obviously, but it looked similar and she liked it, take it as a compliment Mum" I said trying not to laugh.

"Lewis's on the Headrow in Leeds that was from, John the salesman at the time had said it was one of the best ones he had ever sold" scoffed Mum, whilst walking into the room to point at said carpet.

Who the fuck remembers a carpet salesman's name, 15 years after the event?

Yes, my Mum!

I had planted the seed, all I needed to do now was stand back and wait for the rug. It took longer than I thought. Carl and I had bets, he said 1 week, and I said three days. It was one week exactly. Mum and Dad called in, unexpectedly the next Saturday afternoon.

"Oh, I knew there was something to tell you, your Dad and I have just been into town and do you remember that old rug we had in the living room? "said Mum

I nearly said oh the one that Pamela copied from ASDA, but I restrained myself.

"Well, we popped into Lewis's Carpet department and there was the dreamiest rug you have ever seen and I told your Dad how amazing it would look in the living room and how it would give the room a new lease of life, well anyway we got it so if you have a need for a rug, your Dad can bring it over next week once our carpet has been cleaned ready for the new one coming" said my Mum trying her best to make it look like she accidently ended up in the carpet department in Lewis's.

Game set and match to me and welcome to my new rug – the highest quality from Lewis's on the Headrow in Leeds you know, as said by John the salesman.

Oh, bless you mother dear, I can get you every time.

So now we had the rug, we were just about set to have our first official gathering for Jane and Dave. I say first, they had been round every week, at least once a week, since we moved in and they helped us quite a bit with the decorating, but this was going to be for drinks and supper – not quite to my mother's standards but it was quite posh.

Chapter 9

So, before I tell you about our meal I will explain just how close we were as a group.

I could go out with Jane for a drink or I could go out with Dave for a drink – they were both my friends and Carl and I loved them both and I think they felt the same. We were inseparable. If one couple was invited somewhere it usually followed by the other being invited, we very rarely went anywhere without the other and we all liked it like that, that's just the way it was.

We spent Christmas together, if not Christmas dinner then definitely at night.

So back to the meal, we had had various telephone calls (you know the things that were plugged in the wall) as to what we would be cooking, Jane and Dave were doing pudding etc, so we seemed all set.

Garlic mushrooms and crusty bread to start, easy and can be made beforehand.

Carl decided we had to have steak then with all the trimmings – he was in charge of that as I am not very good with raw meat fnar fnar!

Pudding – well Jane and Dave said they were making it which to me means they would bring it with them well they did but still in its packet / raw form.

Jelly to melt and re set, strawberries to cut up, custard to make and cream to whisk!! What were they like – they did bring after eights though, so all is forgiven.

My Mum would have had a fit a) at the menu and b) the lack of organisation.

Our motto, in most things in life was and still is "Just wing it."

Meal over and waiting for the jelly to set, we got talking about weddings. I still felt too young and wanted to wait until Carl had qualified, but Jane and Dave were all set and wanted to get married soon.

As we were talking, I could see that Dave kept going in the kitchen and was making sure the trifle was coming along, personally I thought we would forget all about it and find it somewhere in the morning but as we sat chatting and drinking he kept checking on it and doing the next layer.

Finally, it was all ready and he came in quite triumphant, carrying it like a Gold Medal, at the Olympics but adamant that Jane had to have the first dish.

We sat eating when Jane screamed and started jumping about, I thought she was having an eppi but unbeknown to us, Dave had placed an engagement ring in her dish of trifle!!!! She said yes obviously, well screamed it repeatedly. You see we are close- who else is there on the night someone gets proposed to. We were thrilled for them both and obviously carried on celebrating until the very early hours!!

Laid in bed that night /morning Carl asked me if I was jealous and I can honestly say I wasn't, I wasn't bothered about that yet, as I said earlier, I wanted us to be more settled with Carl's qualifications before we did anything like that.

The planning of their engagement party was mad!!! My Mum and Marie were in full flow, poor Dave's Mum didn't get a look in, not that she was that bothered as you can't drink as much when you are planning, and she was quite happy to let others sort it and pay for it.

It was all booked for a few weeks' time, at the same place as my 18th with the same caterers but now with a new and very improved menu – cooked joints of meat and salads and cheeses now you know no bloody curled up sarnies, but Mark had insisted on Pork Pies – "you can't have a do without a good pork pie" he had scoffed much to Marie and Margo's disgust!

Invitations sorted and sent, caterers booked, decorations and DJ sorted, now just shopping for our outfits.

Straight into town for clothes shopping, Chelsea Girl and Wallis for Jane and I and Lewis's and Scofield Centre for the oldies and numerous coffee stops for a lovely milky coffee and a bun – well it must be done!

Do you remember the cafes in town, usually run by Italians that did the best milky coffee, I'm guessing they were olden days lattes??!!

Anyway, we all managed to get suited and booted and finally we made our way home.

Chapter 10

The day of the engagement party. Now I thought my Mum could be over the top, but she had nothing on Marie – jeez she was out of control. It was more like a Royal Wedding than an engagement party.

Jane and Dave weren't allowed to see each other the night before, which meant a full 24 hours for them, which was a lot. My Mum and I had to be at their house for 5 for hair and make-up and photos. Off we went, Dad dropped us off and decided to bid a hasty retreat once he saw the pandemonium ensuing.

Marie was in a right flap, making sure everyone was there, that Jane had her photographs taken whilst she was getting ready, which wasn't really going according to plan as Jane kept having a sneaky cig and the photographer kept telling Marie – she wasn't impressed. Then the hairdresser rang to say she had a flat tyre so poor Mark was sent out to help her.

The make-up woman did Jane first and I am not being funny, but she looked like a clown, she was clearly from the "more is more" school of beauty. So as not to offend Marie, Jane decided to lock herself in the bathroom and try and salvage the mess the make-up woman had made.

I told her quite politely, once I had seen what she had done to Jane, that I was funny with different make up and would prefer her time be spent on Marie.

"But I could do wonders for you, make you look a proper bobby dazzler" sang the make-up woman. She had one of those very sing songy voices that got right on your tit ends after 3 minutes!

So, this continued for the next hour, as we watched the make-up woman (I didn't talk to her for long enough to find out her name) slap more and more foundation and concealer and powder on Marie and this was way before contouring even existed – maybe she invented it – she was no Kim K that is for sure.

To be fair, she did a good job on Marie, so much so my Mum decided she could do her. I think she only did this, so she could say she had had it professionally done but again it did look ok, little bit heavy on the old saggy eyes but ok non the less.

So now just the hairdresser, she had finally arrived, looking like she had crawled through a hedge backwards, not a very good advert if you ask me and I thought it was her tyre that was flat, did she get a new one from the middle of said hedge?

Mark just needed a quick wash and a splash of Brut and he was ready, well ready to make another pot of tea and have another cig.

Janes hair looked lovely, she had thick dark hair, naturally wavy and she hated it so the hairdresser (Yvonne) I know that because she came bustling in   and said "Hi guys, don't fear, Yvonne is here" but with a Y – pronouncing the Y as a Y and not an I as its pronounced usually, said she would blow dry her hair straight.

"I am going to make sure you all go the ball looking

A M A Z Ing "Yes, she said it like that too!!!

Jane done, me done, not much to do with long blonde curly hair really but she messed about with it for a bit and said it looked "FABOLOUS "Not fabulous but FABOLOUS – OK Yvonne!

Marie and my Mum had started on the wine so that was only going to go one way!

At last, all done, make up – done, hair – done, dresses on and I had decided on a nice blue shift dress worn with the obligatory stockings and Jane had gone for a black puffball type dress. As usual we looked amazing!!

Mark was now shouting that the taxis were here, so this was it we were off.

Oh yes one other thing I forgot to mention, Dave had to meet us at the venue, again bad luck to see Jane before the big night !!!!EH???

The room looked amazing, Helium balloons on every table (they wouldn't last the night) you must pop and inhale, it's kind of the rule at a party, the food was all covered up and the DJ Frank was warming up with mine and Janes idols, a bit of Mel & Kim – "Respectable".

Dave and Carl were looking all smart and gorgeous, Carl, in particular, obvs!

I went over" Hi, you look lovely" and as I spoke I inhaled his aftershave -Kouros of course. "You look gorgeous as usual" said Carl and gave me a quick kiss.

"Just think, we will be doing all this again soon" he said with a wink.

Was that a proposal I thought?

Well the night was fantastic, so many people turned up and Frank was pretty good at getting people up to dance, even if he did look like Jimmy Saville's long-lost brother. The food was good, and the beer was cheap, what more could you ask for, oh and I was right, it didn't get much passed 10 before all the balloons had gone and all you could hear was the very high voices and laughter coming from each table.

It really was a fantastic night and it did get me thinking, I was a bit jealous. Jane always seemed to do everything first, apart from buy a house, we had done that first -well a flat, no sorry an apartment!

Carl and I said our thank yous and goodbyes and headed outside to get our taxi. We couldn't share with anyone as we were the only ones that lived in Farsley. Most of the journey was spent in silence as I was daydreaming about how I would want my engagement party or if I even wanted one but then decided that no way would I get away with not having one, not if my Mum had anything to do with it.

Maybe Carl would ask me and soon, after all his work and course was going really well, he was busy designing a house at the moment as part of his course – he had all the graphy paper stuff and different pencils and rulers, the round ones and triangle ones, he had the lot, very clever my Carl but only because he was studying and working, he was always busy on a night doing is Uni stuff.

Chapter 11

Thursday night, we had just finished a lovely tea of Chicken Kiev, thanks to Mr Fulton and new potatoes and I thought we were going to have a nice night watching TV but no, Carl had to work on his design for his house, so there was only one thing to do.

"Can I have some of that graph paper please and a pencil" I asked.

"Yes, help yourself" said Carl looking puzzled.

Well I thought this is going on for a few more weeks, so if you can't beat them, join them. I had seen what Carl had done and he had talked me through every minute detail, it's not like anyone would ever see it and it would mean I could design my dream house, our Forever House, down to every detail, so that is what I did.

It was detached, obviously, and had an amazing garden, that wrapped round all the house, some bits with rockery, some with patio and some with grass, for the kids.

I wasn't really bothered about the garden, it was more what was inside that I was interested in. I planned the look of the house first. It would be traditional looking, but I wanted a big front door, a double door and rounded.

There were some near the park in Horsforth and our family always called them the keyhole houses, as their doorways looked like keyholes. I didn't want it to look like that though, just big double doors.

A very large bay window was a must with roof tiles on it.

a) Because when I was little, my Dad and I used to go to the shop and on the way back we would have a quiz about our street and one of the questions he once asked me was "which house on our street had tiles on their bay window" and it was ours, it was the only one on the street and I loved that, so I would incorporate that into my "Forever House".

b) Because I always wanted a window seat and the large bay windows would allow that.

I had always pictured sitting on one reading, or watching the birds, feeding the children or just day dreaming, so again that was a must.

The windows would be diamond leaded, not like Mum and Dads house, they had the traditional and original leaded windows from the 50's, very nice, but not for my house.

Ivy would also grow up the side but not a lot, just a bit, so it looked very country. The house would be painted white with that bobbly stuff, I have no idea what it is called and really not that bothered with that detail, but I know what I mean.

There would also be a beautiful chimney stack on top because of course, we would have coal fires, again they work very well with the idea of a large window seat.

I can see me now, sat sitting on said seat – jeez talk about "she sells sea shells on the sea shore" I think I've just invented another!

"She was sat sitting on said seat" I thought that was quite good!

Yes so, I can see me sat on the window seat, with a roaring log / coal fire happily burning away and keeping our house warm, whilst I read poetry or one of the greats – I have no idea what one of the greats are really and I don't suppose Woman's Weekly counts! But I would sit there, reading or knitting, though I can't knit, my Grandma and my Mum have tried to teach me, but I don't think I am cut out for crafty things, so I will stick to reading.

Yes, I am sat reading a book or magazine, the fire has now burned out and I am freezing, but I still look good on my seat.

Curtains or blinds?? I will obviously go for large (for the large windows, good for letting in the light) heavy curtains with swags and tie backs and the curtains and swags would be different but complimentary colours. Blinds, I have decided as the windows would be amazing and it would be a shame to cover them with nets, even the café nets would spoil them, before I go on I am sure you are thinking an architect really would not need to go to all this detail, surely that would be a designer that would do the interior but humour me, if I am drawing my forever house – I am, in my imagination, going to decorate and furnish it as I like, so bear with me, this will be a long chapter.

The hallway will be very light, with a telephone table for the telephone (why is this language so literal, what else is a telephone table going to be used for?)

A window at the side to let in the light, a coat stand – quite big items to have in this area, it shows standing within the community (Well that's what my Mum said, so it must be true) also coat hooks, Jesus Margo, we are right up there with royalty if we have a coat stand and coat hooks! One thing we wouldn't have is a bloody wooden box at the side of the telephone for your money, when you have used the phone! What the hell is all that about??? Every household had one and I don't think anyone ever used them – call it a novelty item, well novelty or not I WON'T be having one.

The floor, I think would be a nice patterned carpet, very thick and spongy to walk on, with a heavy-set pattern, again one of my Mum's sayings, you couldn't have too much pattern in a carpet if it was very good quality. It would sweep up the stairs which obviously would be just off to the side of the hall.

From the hall you would arrive at the dining room. Now this would be lovely, obviously. A large round dining table would sit in the middle of the room and seat 6 people, there would also be a sideboard that housed not only a record player and Hi Fi but a drinks cabinet too and an array of Edinburgh Crystal glasses for all occasions.

A fireplace and a couple of comfy chairs would be to the right of the table and a built-in cupboard at the side to house all the amazing crockery that we would use in this room and not forgetting, the hostess trolley, that would be at the side, ready for action whenever required.

It would be painted very modern with a Habitat vibe, airy and new.

The kitchen – Oh where to start here, definitely red and white, I love a modern kitchen.

The study would have a lot of box shelving, probably in black or white and a white desk with a leather swivel chair.

Four bedrooms and each of them would have their own theme, the master bedroom would be very opulent and spacious with an en- suite bathroom and a shower cubicle.

The spare bedrooms would be very hotel like, and everything matching, possibly Laura Ashley for these, quite country and a total contrast to the rest of the house.

The bathroom would be tiled everywhere and there would be at least one step up to the bath area, to give it that sunken feeling, where you step up to the bath but then step down into it, you know what I mean.

This became a regular occurrence, when Carl was working on his design, so was I. I loved to daydream about it. It had a real opulence about it but a very simple design from the outside. People would see it from afar, obviously as it would have loads of land around it and admire the simpleness but be in awe at its grandeur.

Chapter 12

So, things were going well with Carl and me. Our flat was looking lovely and his course was nearing the end and my forever house was complete. Well the drawing of it.

We still saw Jane and Dave and they were now busy organising their wedding. Obviously, Carl was to be best man and I was Chief Bridesmaid.

Part of me wished it was me getting married but we weren't even engaged, we had too much going on. Carl was busy working more hours, as his course was nearly finished and to be fair his boss Bob or Big Bob as he was known, was really encouraging and a really nice bloke, we had got really close to him.

Big Bob really was a nice bloke, I would say he was in his late 50's, widowed and no children. He had taken Carl under his wing when he first met him. I think he thought of him as the son he never had.

One night whilst Bob was at our house, he told me his life story. Fairly easy to do I suppose, after a bottle and a half of wine. He explained how he had met his late wife June, they had been school sweethearts and married whey they were both just 18. Bob had come from an uncaring family and couldn't wait to move out whilst June was an only child from a very privileged background, but also couldn't wait to be married and buy a house with Bob.

They had an ideal marriage at first, beautiful home that they both worked on, and Bob still lived in to this day, all the latest gadgets, a stone fire place that was the best for miles around, as Bob had built it, with various little nooks and crannies for all the Lladro that June collected.

It was perfect until the time they decided that they would quite like to try for a family. This was not going to happen.

As Bob explained, they had tried for many a year and it just wasn't meant to be. No testing really in those days and as Bob put it "If we were meant to have kids then kids we would have had."

It was very sad, as a loving couple you just presume that you will have a family and unfortunately for so many people this is a very precious gift not always offered.

He filled up, did Bob, when he said when Carl appeared at his building site all those years ago, he felt like he had gained a son and now that Carl and I were together he felt he had now also gained a daughter. He was a massive part of our lives and had now started getting invites to all our family gatherings.

 He really was a top bloke and we thought of him as part of our family. The childless years went by for Bob and June, but they enjoyed travel and had been to so many exotic and faraway places and had a beautiful home, built from scratch by Bob and lovingly decorated and nurtured by June.

The years went by for Bob and June and Bob kept on building his empire and employing more and more people and June kept house, baked and cooked. That's what she was very good at apparently, a true home maker and she would have made the best mother.

It was late September the year June turned 50 and Bob had been working away on and off for a few weeks. "It was bloody freezing for a September and reet wet. I'd been working away solid for a week with the lads and decided enough were enough and I were off home to my June" said Bob.

"I don't know what made me do it, it was late, and I just thought bugger it, life's too short to be buggering about, to be cold and wet and away from my June so I packed up and pissed off. It was a reet drive home, all I could think about were seeing my June and getting a reet warm bath. I remember singing all the way home. I felt like I had been away for years and I had that feeling you get in your belly when your reet excited abart sommat. As I pulled into the drive I noticed there were no lights on. Strange, as June hadn't mentioned she was going anywhere when I spoke to her yesterday, but I carried on and walked into the house.

As I walked in I was calling her name, I don't know why, just habit I suppose and I flicked on each light in every room until I got to the kitchen and that is when I saw her.

My June, laid face down, in the kitchen, with the tea towel still in her hand." said Bob.

"I didn't get it, why wasn't she moving, what was she doing? I knelt at the side of her and turned her over. She looked beautiful, very peaceful but her lips were blue. I couldn't leave her now. I picked her up and I carried her to the sun room and laid her on the settee in there.

I knew I had to call someone, the ambulance, police whatever but I knew I had to do it quickly not because they might be able to help her, as I knew that was too late, but so that I could have time with her before they took her away. I knew she was gone but I just needed to be alone with her for a while. I can't remember who I rang but as soon as I put the phone down I opened the front door, put on the outside light and went and sat with my June. I told her how much I loved her, I cried and asked her why had she left me, what had I done to make this happen? We sat there together, just me and June for what felt like 2 mins because before I knew it there was a policewoman and ambulance men at the side of me asking me what had happened" said Bob, visibly upset.

He continued "as I spoke to the policewoman, she carefully moved me to another room, so the ambulance could work on her I suppose.

I explained it all, how I had spoken to her the day before, she seemed fine, she was always fit and healthy and how I had come home today as I was fed up and needed to see June and be at home with her when I had come home and found her on the kitchen floor.

She was lovely and before I knew it, I saw one of the ambulance men come in, tap the police woman on her shoulder and motion her to come in the other room. I knew deep down that my June had gone but there is always that little glimmer of hope that they had saved her. It wasn't meant to be.

My June had gone, and I was now sat in my kitchen whilst Mandy the policewoman made me a strong cuppa. We were waiting for the undertakers to take my June away."

Bob paused and got himself together, before he continued.

"Mandy had told me that it looked like June had had a heart attack, that is what the ambulance men had said, and we just had to wait for the funeral directors to take her away. I couldn't believe it, how she had gone but I did find out that she had heart failure and she always had and that it was only a matter of time. She had died, she was gone and what was I going to do now" sniffed Bob.

Bob had really poured his heart out to us that night, told me how he still talked to her and how she would have loved me and Carl, like he did and that was why he wanted to give Carl and me every opportunity in life he could, for our future and he would live his life through us, helping us where he could.

I presumed he meant giving Carl a job and hours to suit his college etc, but he had high hopes for Carl, he wanted him eventually designing and building houses with Bob's help he said the sky was the limit.

I think it really, really helped Bob talking so openly like that and I am a good listener. I can't imagine he has anyone to be able to do that with.

Men aren't known for their openness and showing their feelings, they don't really talk about their feelings much do they? They keep it bottled in, so I was glad Bob had finally got it all out.

We talked and talked until the early hours of the morning, he was telling us both the fun he and June had got up to on their far away trips to the States and Australia and the many luxury cruises they had had. He still filled up when he talked about the lack of family he had. He thinks his brother is still alive, but he was much older than Bob and had moved out of the family home not long after Bob was 3, so they didn't have a relationship at all.

As I mentioned earlier Bobs family life was not what most people are used to. He told us how his mother and father continually told him he was a mistake, a drunken mistake that would cost them for the rest of their lives because he wasn't planned but his mother hadn't realised she was pregnant and only knew once she had gone into labour.

She was hoping for a child free life as Bob's brother was a teenager when Bob was born, and she thought he would be ready to move out in a few years but, on the plus side, he was now working and bringing money into the family.

I say family but not family as I am lucky enough to know.

They really did sound dreadful and not caring at all which is so sad and quite unusual as Bob was a very kind and considerate man, unusual when you have had such a bad upbringing, but I guess you either follow suit or go the other way and luckily for Bob, he wasn't bitter at all and turned the other cheek and went the complete opposite way to them.

We eventually poured Bob into a taxi to take him home in the early hours of the morning.

As I laid in bed that night, I realised just how precious life is, you never know what is around the corner and you really should live each day as if it's your last.

Unbeknown to me at the time, Carl too was thinking the same, in fact so much so, he had a plan up his sleeve and all he needed was a bit of help from Bob.

Chapter 13

It was nearing my birthday and we had all decided to go out for a meal. The usual, me, Carl, his Mum and Dad and sisters, my sister and James, Jane and Dave, My Grandma and of course Big Bob and my Mum and Dad.

We were going to try a new Italian that had opened in the park. The Roman Garden, I think it was called.

There had always been a restaurant there, but this was new owners and of course my Mum had to get in there first to make an impression and make sure they knew her, for next time she went. They would know her name and they would make a fuss.

There wasn't a lot of planning gone into the meal as everyone's time was currently taken up with the planning of the wedding of Jane and Dave. So much so her Mum and Dad had taken off for a week to get away from it all I think.

So, it was arranged, we would all meet at the restaurant for 8 o'clock. My Dad wasn't picking us up, as he usually did because he wanted a drink, so we said we would meet everyone there. Even Bob was making his own way there.

Carl was on edge all day, in fact if I am perfectly honest, he was a bit of an arse all day, but I wasn't going to let him spoil my birthday meal. Today was about me, NOT Jane or Dave, but ME. ME ME ME ME ME, so he could stick his arsey mood up his arse and off I went to get a bath.

I could hear a lot of banging about but chose to ignore it and slip under the hot water and stayed there, as long as I could.

On finally getting out, I went straight to the bedroom to dry my hair and start getting ready. To be honest if I hadn't gone to the bedroom from the bathroom there wasn't really much of a choice of other rooms, kitchen or living room, so bedroom it had to be.

I was finally ready with a good half hour to spare. I checked and re checked myself, not bad girl, even if I do say so myself.

As I walked into the living room there he was, my little arsey Carl looking all gorgeous with a gift in his hand. I would say it was A4, but paper sizes aren't really my thing, but it wasn't massive, and it wasn't tiny.

"What's that" I said pointing to the gift.

"Well it's not for me and as there is no one else here, I would say it's for you, call it an early birthday pressie" said Carl beaming at me.

"Ooooh let me see" I said as I took it off him and started unwrapping it.

"Oh my god, that is fantastic" I exclaimed as I saw MY FOREVER HOUSE, the one I had designed, all professional like and here it was all properly drawn up and in a frame with the words "OUR FOREVER HOUSE, OUR DREAM, ONE DAY"

It was perfect and so thoughtful, and it looked amazing now it was all properly drawn up, a real blueprint. I ran over to kiss him, when he got up and said, there's something else outside for you and he pointed to the door.

This just gets better I thought and ran to the door.

Outside in the porch, was what looked like a box with a cover on it. I pulled the cover off to discover OUR HOUSE, perfectly made as a doll's house.

The detail was stunning, and it was painted white just as I had pictured. I turned to look at Carl and I started to cry, at the sheer thoughtfulness of it all. This was something we had done together, over the last few months, as Carl was working on his, I was working on this, with his help.

"It is absolutely perfect, and I couldn't ask for a better gift, I absolutely love it" I said still crying and I flung my arms round him.

As he pulled me away he just said "open the door"

I was guessing he meant the doll's house door and as I did, I took out a little box and on opening it, inside was the most amazing sight ever. A diamond and sapphire ring, an engagement ring, I was hoping. I turned around to find Carl bent down on one knee and he muttered "will you marry me?"

"Oh my god, oh my god, oh my god, Yes, Yes Yes" I squealed, as I threw myself at him, causing us both to drop to the ground, when I realised he hadn't put the ring on my finger.

We both got up and he placed it gently on my finger, watching me, fixing me with his eyes all the while. God he was a sexy bastard!

"I cannot believe this, this is the best day of my life, who knows??? Oh god, I can't wait to tell everyone. I can do it tonight when everyone will be there, this is amazing" and I just ran from room to room and back again unsure what to do first!

"There is only your Dad that knows, I asked him last week for your hand in marriage" said Carl.

"I thought it was only right and I knew you would love the surprise and with us going out tonight for your birthday meal, I thought it would be the perfect opportunity to tell everyone together" said Carl still beaming.

"You, my love, are the best boyfriend, oops I mean Fiancée ever" I said and kissed him hard on the lips

"Right come on then Mr, we need to go tell everyone" I shouted, and we laughed and got ready to go to meet everyone.

I only had about 20 minutes to get used to the news before the taxi had arrived to take us to the Italian, so I was unsure how I was going to tell everyone.

I knew for a fact my Dad wouldn't have spilt the beans, so I was very excited but nervous at the same time.

When we arrived, there was only my parents and Carl's and my Grandma, so I decided to get the three ladies on their own and break the news.

I got them into the toilet, of all places and just put out my left hand.

It was my Grandma who spoke first, the Mums were just mute with their mouths open smiling. "OOOOOHHH you have got engaged, I hope it's to Carl" said my Grandma.

Laughing I replied, "who else would it be Grandma" and we all hugged and laughed and cried.

Why do women cry when they are sad and cry when they are happy?? And we wonder why men don't understand us.

The three ladies were over the moon. "Right well, this is a double celebration tonight" said my Mum and shouted as if to my Dad, "Champagne to celebrate".

I think she was more than chuffed, not only was she happy for myself and Carl but also the Italians would certainly remember her now!!!

As we got back into the main part of the restaurant, everyone else had arrived and were all sat at the table.

My Mum walked over to my Dad, whispered in his ear and went to take her place. My Dad, I found out earlier, was one step ahead and had ordered champagne for the table to be brought out when he gave the head waiter the nod.

This he did as we all sat down, my Dad stood up and said

"Tonight, ladies and gents, we are not only celebrating my baby girl's birthday, but I have the great honour in telling you all, that approximately one hour ago, Clare said yes to becoming Carl's wife."

The head waiter had already handed out a glass of champagne to everyone and one for himself and he said, "Cheers to the happy couple" and everyone cheered and congratulated us.

The champagne and wine were flowing all night. I was pulled from woman to woman to look at the ring and given numerous cuddles and hugs from not only our table, but all the waiters and most of the other guests.

I couldn't go to the toilet without some random woman saying "Congratulations" I felt very special and was very much in love, not only with Carl but with my beautiful engagement ring.

Carl was the same, handshakes, congrats and hugs all night.

I finally got my Dad on my own and just said "I love you Dad and thank you for saying yes and keeping it a secret"

"I love you too sweetheart and I wouldn't have had it any other way, I know you love surprises, like I always say, I know you better than you know you" said my Dad, pulling me in for a hug and kissing me on the head.

Jane and Dave were also thrilled, though we did tell them straight away we would not be getting married or planning anything until they had got married. Even though, for a split second, Jane and I did contemplate a joint wedding.

We explained to everyone that we wouldn't be having a big engagement party, it was something Carl and I had previously discussed, as we were saving for a house and he was working all hours, but my Mum flatly refused to allow that and said she would hold a "Supper" at her house to celebrate.

By supper,

she means a party, but she obviously wouldn't just call it a party – that would be far too common!

So that was agreed, although Carl and I didn't have much say in it.

A Supper at the parents would be marvellous – is all Carl, myself, Jane and Dave could say for the rest of the night, silently taking the piss out of my Mum.

Now even though Bob helped Carl with the drawings of our house and the making of the doll's house, he too had no idea that Carl was going to propose. He came over to us both, just before he left and said," I am so proud of you both and so thrilled you are going to be united, legally and this marks the first chapter for the rest of your lives together".

He was very old school was our Bob, we were living in sin and he much preferred it now I had a ring on my finger and he will be even more so and able to sleep at night once I say I DO.

Bless him, he is a little sweetie.

So here we are, all grown up and engaged! It felt very strange but good at the same time. I couldn't wait to go to work on Monday and show off my ring!

Chapter 14

I walked through the main office and straight into the kitchen, I knew most people would be in there having a fag and a coffee before they officially started work, not that they couldn't smoke at their desk because they could, but there is nothing nicer than a chat, a coffee and a fag!

So, in I walked, said my usual "Morning" to everyone that was there and went straight over to the kettle to get my caffeine fix. I hadn't even switched the bloody thing on before Moyra in accounts screamed "Oh my god is that a ring? Are you engaged?"

Everyone gasped and ran over to see if Moyra's suspicion was correct.

As I regaled them all about the night Carl proposed and how he proposed and showed off my ring I suddenly felt very overwhelmed and very grown up but extremely happy at the prospect of spending the rest of my life with my Carl, the man of my dreams.

We didn't get much work done that morning, every time anyone walked down the office Moyra was straight out telling them my news!

Alright Moyra love, pack it in, the MD of Fultons Foods really doesn't give a shit!! Neither does Derek from Life and Pensions, he tutted every time anyone mentioned it, not that I gave a shit about Derek, he was on overweight and over bearing ginger twat that never smiled and I suspected if he wasn't careful would be returned unopened, so to speak, the big fat ginger twat.

No one was going to spoil my mood and I wasn't going to stop talking about it for the sake of Derek or any other fucker come to think of it.

At lunchtime we were all sat in the back, the cool set. Well I say cool, it was mainly just the ladies in accounts, me and the rest of the general team and of course Derek the spaz, sat in the corner with his nose in a book, eating a Thurston's pasty and chain smoking.

You would think he was enthralled in his paper but mention something he didn't agree with and he was straight in there joining in on the PRIVATE CONVERSATION!

I knew he was always listening. so just to piss him off a bit more I turned the conversation back to the engagement and the ring and the Supper at the parents. Yes Derek, stick that in your big fat ginger pipe!

My supervisor had nipped out before we all congregated in the kitchen and just as we were discussing the wedding (now this really was pissing Derek off as he knew this could go on for years) she came in and handed me "Wedding Magazine" for the wedding of your dreams.

"Here, I thought this might get your juices flowing for the forthcoming event of the century" said Anne, with a little giggle and nodding over at Derek.

"Oh, thank you, oh god that's fantastic, I can start and make a scrap book of all the things I would love for my wedding, now where to start? The dress, the venue, the invitations, the theme, the menu? Oh god this could take a while" I scoffed and I too nodded over to Derek.

Every minute of every day had been taken up with Jane and Dave's wedding and I had promised them that we wouldn't start on ours till way after theirs, after all, I had only been engaged a few days, but I couldn't help it.

I kept buying more and more magazines and I would sit at night whilst Carl was finishing off his college work and I would cut out the dresses and invitations from bridal magazines and carefully stick them in my "WEDDING OF THE YEAR" scrap book.

The plans for the Supper at the parents were going very well. Well I think they were, I didn't really have a say in it, but I do know that my Mum was thrilled with her latest bit of news.

"Hi, its Mum, now are you sat down? If not, I need you to sit down straight away, have you done it? Are you sat down? Well anyway, sat down or not I just have to tell you this before I burst. You are not going to believe what I am about to tell you Clare, you really aren't. Brian, I am just about to tell Clare the news, don't you think she will love it when I tell her" screeched my Mum

You get the picture here that basically my Mum very rarely ever called our house and if she did it was usually a twenty-minute phone call, with her building up the tension, making sure you were suitably excited, and she would eventually break the news and tell you what she could have told you in one short sentence, but that was not how she worked. It was all about the tension building and you knew you had a good ten minutes of this before she got to the point, so as she started, I mouthed at Carl that it was Mum, he rolled his eyes and we both went to the kitchen to make a coffee, knowing full well the kettle will have boiled before she had even got to the start of the point of the call.

I left it a good five minutes before I retrieved the phone receiver from the telephone table and held it to my ear (the phone that is, not the table) and sensed she was getting near to the crucial point, so I sat down and motioned to Carl to bring me my coffee.

We were both huddled round the phone listening to her going on and on when she finally said "soooooooooooooo, Gino, my friend, you know the lovely manager at the restaurant in the park, you know the one you got engaged in" screeched my Mum on full pelt.

Now hang on a minute there mother, one, YOUR FRIEND! you met him once, two I didn't get engaged there I was technically already engaged when I got to said place and three, just get on with it woman! Obviously, I didn't say any of this out loud, but I was thinking it very loudly.

"Sooooooooooo, wellllllllllllll," she continued

For fucks sake SPIT IT OUT WOMAN! Thinking not speaking obviously!

She continued "He has agreed to come over to our house and cook for us at your engagement supper, how exciting is that" screeched the mother yet again

"But I thought it was a bit of a party, a few drinks and a few nibbles not a full three course meal" I said

"It is darling, when I say he's coming to cook at ours, what I really mean is, he is going to prepare it and bring it over, he is doing the catering, isn't that just the best news in the whole wide world?" screeched Mum.

Well for a start, what she was saying is he does outside catering and he is doing some for us. The way she sees it is he is now her man servant and very excited to be asked to do such an event, in fact, it's like saying if you buy Uncle Bens rice, he has actually come over (once he has picked the rice) and he has added it into salty water in your kitchen, therefore he has cooked for you.

This woman gets worse, and mother dear, it is very exciting but, Best News in the whole world – really -maybe the Argentinians surrendering would be much better news not the fact that the local Italian does outside catering.

So, on she went for a good 25 minutes and at the end I put Carl on, as she was going to tell him the whole story all over again until he said he had heard it all. Yes, it was fabulous but if he was just doing pizza couldn't we just go to Fultons and buy some frozen ones to cook at home.

Cue the picture of a volcano erupting.

Time stood still for what felt like an eternity. Jesus Carl what have you done, have you not learnt anything these past few years?

I took the phone off him and before she had time to speak said "He is joking Mum, you know how he likes to joke and he knows it's not just pizza but that it's all his family's favourites from all over Italy" I said very quickly.

Mum was quite flustered at this and not sure what to say so she bid her goodbyes and hung up.

"Good one dick head" I scoffed as we started laughing.

"Get the car keys, we are now going to have to go around and show how excited we are and let her go on and on because if not my poor Dad will get it in the neck for ever more" I said

"Shall we call and get pizza on the way" laughed Carl

We got to my Mums and she was secretly thrilled to see us, she knew, I knew, how she worked, and she was thrilled that I had taken the hint and not really shown enough enthusiasm on the phone, so a home visit was in order.

"Oh, how lovely to see you both I wasn't expecting you to come all this way over, do you want a drink and maybe something to eat?" Sang my mother knowing full well she had won yet again.

"Yes, that's lovely thank you, now tell us all about the catering for the supper" said Carl, through gritted teeth.

He was learning! We sat for over three hours listening to her go on and on, luckily, we did get fed and watered and there was a visit from my sister and Grandma during this time, which was lovely, but it did mean we had to hear the story right from the beginning again, building the tension, setting the scene etc. So much so, that my sister and Grandma only lasted an hour, made an excuse to leave and left and I am sure I saw my Grandma laugh at me as she was walking out of the door!

Chapter 15

Tonight, we went to Bob's for tea. We took it in turns every week, one week he came to us, the next we went to him. It wasn't out of necessity but because we wanted to. He was such a lovely and kind man, we loved spending time with him.

Bob was a good cook but never followed recipes and made things up as he went along. If he liked two certain things he would put them together and make a name up for this invention. Apparently, this is what he used to do to June all the time.

Bob has told us before what an amazing cook and baker June was, but she also loved that he liked to cook for her and she would laugh at his various concoctions.

Tonight, we were having bolognaise bake which was basically cottage pie with bolognaise instead of mince and veg. Like I said earlier, Bob loves mash and he loves spaghetti bolognaise but felt mash and spaghetti might be pushing it a bit.

You had to love him, and you never quite knew what to expect when you went to his for a meal.

We finished his bolognaise bake and I went to help him in the kitchen to wash up whilst Carl played with Bob's new puppy Scamp.

I forgot to mention Scamp. Bob had decided a few months ago that he wanted a bit of company at home, he still hadn't got used to coming in to an empty house, even after all this time. Also, as Carl was working full time for him now, as his course had finished, Bob had decided to do less hours, so a dog would be perfect, and Scamp was perfect.

He was a Heinz 57, bit of Terrier in him and not sure what else. He was a decent size dog and very loyal and loveable.

As Bob and I washed up we chatted, as we did, about his business and I said that now he was working less he could think about taking travelling up again, but he wasn't having any of it.

"My days of travel died the day my June died, I saw all I wanted with her and I don't want to see anymore without her" he said in a quiet sad voice.

"Scamp and I are alreet here on our own, going on our walks and trips to Filey, he loves it at Filey does our Scamp and he especially likes the cockles and mussels" said Bob

We carried on until we had washed, dried and put all the dinner pots and pans away and made a coffee for us all and went to join Carl and Scamp in the Sun room.

Now since Bob told me about Junes death, every time I went into the sun room I couldn't but help picture her laid dead on the settee, needless to say, I always sat in a chair.

Carl and Bob chatted for a while about work and I played with Scamp and then the conversation changed to our impending engagement supper.

We told Bob all about my Mum and her plans and we didn't half laugh as Bob did a very good impression of my Mum, without being nasty, but it wasn't something he would have dared do in front of her.

The soiree was the following Saturday and we checked Bob was ok to get there and told him the times and dress code.

I know, I know, but yes there was a dress code, it was at my Mums for god sake, of course there was etiquette to be followed.

After all the arrangements were made, Carl and I said our goodbyes and headed off home. Half way home Carl veered off the normal route and took me down New Road Side and turned down onto Victoria Walk.

"What are we doing here" I asked very confused

"I am showing you our new home" said Carl

And as he did so he, pulled up outside number 37. A beautiful semi-detached house on a beautiful treelined cul de sac.

"What? Our? When? How? Eh?" I spluttered.

"Bob said it was time we got a bigger place, something to get our teeth into and because I have finished my course and working for him fulltime, it means he can work part time, so he thinks we deserve a bit of a bonus" sang Carl, ecstatic that he could finally tell and show me.

"He bought us a house" I screamed.

"No silly arse, but he gave us the deposit, we just have to sell ours now, we have put an offer in on this and it's been accepted. I contacted the estate agents last week and the board should go up tomorrow and they think they have a buyer for ours already. Because Bob is helping us, we can afford to put the flat up a bit cheaper, so it sells" said Carl.

"Oh right, well it's all sorted" I said, a little miffed that I hadn't been consulted at all.

"You don't sound too pleased" said Carl.

"I'm sorry I am, it is just a massive shock, I didn't even think about moving yet but you're right and this house looks perfect" I said and with that I turned and gave him a massive kiss. He really was amazing at surprises and I really couldn't wait to look inside the house.

Carl explained that the location is perfect, the size of the house is perfect, for now, but can be extended and the inside is immaterial really as he can change it to what I want anyway.

So that was that, it looked like we were moving – what a day – the impending supper at the parents was just days away and I really had no idea what to expect and now I have just found out I am moving to a house, I didn't know even existed until about 5 minutes ago.

With that we drove home, and I went to bed to start planning my, oops sorry, our new house. It wasn't the house, it was pretty perfect, but because I hadn't seen inside, it was quite difficult to visualise. Tomorrow morning, I would ring the estate agents and make an appointment to look round. To sleep I went with a smile on my face.

Also, I couldn't wait to tell my family and Sunday would be the perfect time as we were all invited for Sunday lunch at Mum and Dads.

I did eventually get to look round the house and it was pretty perfect, just the way it was set out. You walked in through the front door, to the right was a lounge with a lovely stone fireplace and a large bookcase to the right and shelving to the left, this will be taken out and a stereo put in there. It had beautiful bay windows, not big enough for a seat but beautiful anyway. Out into the hall, room for the obligatory telephone table and coat stand and room for coat hooks too. Stairs to the right and straight on into the dining room with a pantry and a little galley kitchen. The dining room looked out onto a patio and I thought the kitchen was a little small but could easily be extended.

Upstairs were three good size bedrooms and a large bathroom.

Small garden to the front, with beautiful rose bushes. I just hoped they would be white and NOT red – we do not have RED ROSES IN THIS HOUSE, one of my Dad's pet hates – red you see, is for Manchester/ Lancashire and as we are Leeds and Yorkshire born and bred, it's the white rose all the way.

Large driveway and garage, outside, obviously and a beautiful back garden with the patio as I mentioned earlier, a few steps down on to a large lawn and then then onto what looked like an allotment.

I was smiling all the way round the house, this my friends, was going to be a perfect home for me, my husband to be and at least two children, a girl and a boy. Perfect.

By the time Carl got home that night, I nearly knocked him over as I ran at him to give him a kiss. I explained I had been to the house and loved every inch of it and that it didn't need much doing, only decorating really and maybe a new kitchen and ooh yes we would have to extend the kitchen, its tiny, but the garden was perfect and the rooms were a decent size and there was a perfect place for the stereo and on and on I went when Carl said "steady on Margo" to which we howled with laughter, I was turning into my Mum.

Once we had composed ourselves, Carl simply said "I'm glad you love it because I have just accepted an offer on this place, the estate agent has a buyer lined up and we move in about 6 weeks."

"Six weeks, oh my god that's about the time of Janes wedding" I said, fear in my voice.

"And? The wedding is a day, we can work round it, it's not like we have a lot to move from here, we will throw most of it and buy new for the house. My wage has gone up with a bang now I'm fulltime, it will be fine, don't worry" said Carl soothingly whilst holding me close to reassure me.

So that was that, I was moving, and the wedding would be fine and now all we had to do was get through the supper at the parents.

Well to say I was apprehensive about the "Supper at the parents" I have to say it was a fantastic night. My Mum really had pulled out all the stops. Not too many people were invited, because although we said close friends and family only, both Carl and I were surprised that there was only a handful of people there we had never met before.

John and Karen from the Golf club (obviously) never met them before, Ken and Carol from the cricket club (never met them before) and Carlos and his wife Julietta whom I had met briefly, as they served me my food at the restaurant in the park - No, they weren't the owners (he was too busy on a Saturday night obviously) but they were his family, supposedly, and Italian, again supposedly (very important to have foreign friends as my Mum says) also not sure about the Italian bit as I'm sure I went to school with her and she was broad Yorkshire and not called Julietta, but I wasn't going to burst Mums bubble, not just yet anyway! They were there of course to serve, well I think that's why??!!!

The food was amazing and plentiful. Italian and a bit of Spanish thrown in. I'm guessing that was my Mums contribution (the Sangria was a dead giveaway, as my Mum always made it following her first visit to Spain. Tossa de Mar.) I know, I chuckled at the thought of my Mum there too, it was her favourite to take to friend's gatherings "Its SANGRIA, ITS SPANISH" she used to enunciate it as though all her friends were a bit simple and obviously not as well travelled or cultured as her.

Apart from that, it was lovely, she had tastefully decorated the gazebo in the garden with balloons and banners (none in the house, no bluetac allowed on her very exclusive flock wallpaper).

She had a cake made (again obviously it was made for her) baking and my Mum, didn't go hand in hand, and then she made my Dad give a speech.

It was lovely and from the heart and I think he got a bit emotional (it's a big thing, I would imagine, next step, they get married and move away, only I had already done that) until my Mum shouted "That's enough now let's raise a glass to the happy couple. Putting my Dad right in his place as usual.

Jane and Dave were there, so obviously the conversation turned to them and the wedding, which I wasn't bothered about and to be honest I couldn't wait actually. Not just for the wedding but we had the hen night first and what was making it all the better was my Mum and Marie were in attendance and the girl who had arranged it all was a friend of Janes from work and had insisted she sorted it as she would be away for the wedding.

Her brother owned a bar in town that would be perfect for it and let's just say, that this friend was not and did not, carry herself as we would. Let's just say she had a heart of gold but was a little bit rough and I couldn't wait to see what she had arranged.

Sue was, shall we say, very ofay with the opposite sex and very comfortable to tell, all who would listen, about her various shenanigans with various men in various bars and pubs around town.

She is what my Mum would call, loose. I am sure whatever it is, will be totally inappropriate for my Mum and Marie!!

The rest of the night went off amazingly, my Grandma was up dancing with Bob a few times (if only she was twenty years younger) they both had a ball and my sister was very quiet as she was heavily pregnant, but she enjoyed the food!

My Mum had said everyone had been asking her what we wanted for an engagement gift and that we were not to worry, she had told them suitable items that we hadn't yet got around to buying. God help us on that one, as the things my Mum said we needed and the things we needed, were two totally different things.

To be fair, we did seem to have received many gifts and Mum had graciously taken them off each guest as they arrived telling people "Thank you so much for your gift, but they will save them to open when they get home."

Which is very true, there is nothing worse than opening a gift in front of someone and having to fain interest and pretend to like it. I think though, the real reason was, so my Mum wasn't left with all the mess and boxes to throw away.

The party was ending, my sister had eaten her way round the food, three times to my knowledge, the Italians had done their job brilliantly and suitably impressed Mums friends and Mum had asked them to leave, once the friends had left. Grandma had been taken home by Bob, not in that way, but he did say he would see her safely home as she had had one or two sherries.

Jane and Dave had gone, as they were up early the following morning, to sample the menu at the hotel where they were having their wedding reception.

In fact, the only ones left, apart from us were Carl's Mum and Dad. Carl's Mum would help tidy and the two Dads would sit back and break open the whisky my Dad kept for such occasions.

Each time he did this he would make Carl join them in a glass and each time he dutifully obliged, as he said he felt like he had been accepted by being offered one and each time when my Dad wasn't looking, he would pour it away as he couldn't stand the stuff. He would keep trying it and allowing the foul-smelling liquid to touch his lips with each lift of the glass, in the hope that it would miraculously disappear.

As all the clearing up was done, the ladies came to join us, them with a glass of well-earned Baileys (keeping up the Mediterranean feel I see mother) and the men and their whiskey.

We sat for quite a while talking about the success of the evening and how this made us all family now almost – I was just waiting for them all to start with the "I really love you shite" that comes out of people's mouths after far too much to drink, when Carl said we had better get off and ordered us a taxi.

We bundled all our gifts into the car and decided we would open them all when we got home, neither of us would be able to wait until the morning we are both too nosey.

We finally got home and took all the gifts out of the taxi, stacked the gifts up in the living room and started to open them.

Some of them clearly were my mother's idea like the plate chargers to warm your plates, the Lazy Susan for your dining table (we didn't have a dining table but I'm sure it will work on the floor) crystal glasses (very 1970's) and the piece de resistance was the bread machine.

The one saving grace was no sign of a pot horse pulling a cart of plastic beer barrels, no sign of a spooky Pierrot Doll picture, not a hint of a crying boy picture and not a glimpse of a picture of a lady with a blue face. The bread machine however, will my friends, be taken back from whence it came and swapped for a fabulous coffee machine. You see not only did my Mum have the cheek to be very specific in what people should buy us, she also insisted on knowing where it was from and receiving a receipt for the item, in the guise that we may already have one and she just hadn't seen it.

Thank god for mothers, as there were quite a few that were to be exchanged and we worked it out, we could get the updated version of the coffee machine we so wanted.

You know the ones that are a smaller version of the ones in the cafes – make fantastic coffees and warm and froth your milk.

So, we were well and truly blessed with our gifts, we had done well and that was just a few more boxes for us to pack up ready for our move.

Chapter 16

The day after the night before.

Mum and Dad had invited us all for Sunday lunch. She hadn't done in it a while with all the engagement and wedding plans, in fact the last time we went was when my sister announced she was having a baby.

It was fantastic news, but part of me wanted it to be me, I don't know why, I wasn't sure if I wanted children, well I did but I hadn't really thought about it seriously until my sister said she was having one.

I had pushed the bad thoughts to the back of my mind and congratulated them both. It was very exciting times and I couldn't wait to be an Auntie

So, this time round, it was me who was going to give my family some exciting news, ok so not quite as exciting as becoming a Mummy but it was exciting none the less.

We sat down to full mashing's Sunday lunch of Roast Beef, Yorkshire Puddings and all the trimmings.

I don't know about you, but in our family, we always had the Yorkshire puddings as a starter? Strange really but there you go.

So, after we had devoured the first two courses (of course that was it, have the Yorkies as a starter and you can say you always have three courses on a Sunday). Mum brought out apple crumble and custard, so I thought I would tell my family my news.

"Erm Carl and I have some news." The silence that followed was deafening.

My Mum had her hand to her mouth in shock, my Dad was just staring and my sister, whom I think had guessed what the news was, just laughed.

"Dear god tell me you are not pregnant with the amount you put away last night young lady" started Mum and off she went on one of her usual rambles.

"MUM I am not pregnant" I shouted to try shut her up.

"Not that I don't want you to be pregnant, of course I do just not now, you're not married yet and you live in a flat" she rambled on and on again.

"MOTHER" I shouted "I know what you mean, don't worry but can I just tell you our news please. We have bought a house and we move in a few weeks" I said.

Relief was written all over hers and my Dad's face. The chatter soon turned to where, when, what etc so after we had told them everything they needed and wanted to know, my Dad came over and congratulated us both with the obligatory pat of the arm.

So that was that, all my family knew and were all really pleased for us and so, after we had cleared away and had a coffee, we bid our farewells and set off to tell Carls Mum and Dad.

We set off via our new home, obviously, and we both just sat outside it, in the car, looking at it. We had to be careful not to scare the people that already lived there, we didn't want them changing their minds and not moving.

After about ten minutes we turned around in the lovely cul de sac, all the while checking out the rest of the houses on the street and then we set off to Carl's Mum and Dads.

I think they thought the same when we told them we had some news. In fact, if I didn't know Carl better, I would say he did it on purpose to wind them up a bit.

They were both really pleased and said they would help in any way they could.

So, we were all set, boxes were starting to be packed, all family told. All there was to do now was get through the hen night and stag night and wait for the wedding, get that done and then we can move.

We had moved the moving in date to the week after Jane and Dave's wedding. It gave us a little longer to pack up and buy a few essentials i.e. the coffee machine!!!

Chapter 17

The Hen night was here at last and me and my Mum and Jane and Marie were all getting a lift into town, to meet the rest of them in one of the pubs there.

We walked into the Dog and Duck and the sight that greeted us can only be described as a giant, luminous pink COCK!

Well it looks like this night is only going to go one way.

"Over ere, Jane, psssst, over ere, ey, what do you think of me outfit eh, thought I'd make sure you see what real men have before you say I do" and with that Sue was in fits of laughter, swaying about and spilling most of her Malibu and coke as she did so.

Mum and Marie's face was a picture !!!!If only I had time to get my camera out of my bag.

Jane did the introductions of the mothers, who were still agog and staring at Sue.

"Ey don't you worry ladies, as I always say before a night out, what happens tonight stays with us and is not discussed out of this group, deal?" spat Sue.

"Erm, well yes of course" spluttered both mothers.

Jane and I gave each other the look, this was going to be hilarious, they really didn't have a clue what to expect although I think the penny might be about to drop.

Sue grabbed a large carrier bag and started dishing out various badges, they said:

Bride to be (but for tonight single and free)

Maid of Honour (Left her honour at home tonight)

Mother of the bride (Tonight sister of the bride and ask no questions)

Friend of the Bride (Tonight she will be anyone you want)

Not bad considering that now you see T shirts emblazoned with "Donna she likes it standing up" or "Michelle she takes it in the Outy".

Back in the early nineties, thankfully you had a few funny badges and a tacky veil, adorned with a few L plates and maybe the odd condom or two.

Talking about tacky veils, Sue didn't disappoint, she plonked the veil, that had condoms stapled on, on Janes head and announced to the pub "This is the bride to be, but she's up for it tonight lads, last night of being single"

Haaaaaaaaaaaaaaaa this just gets better.

A few more people arrived, and the badges were starting to repeat themselves, I'm guessing Sue could only think of a few before she thought, oh fuck it, it'll do.

We had a couple of drinks in there and then Sue announced that it was time to move on to the "Hen Do Propper" I'm guessing she meant her brothers bar.

So, we downed our drinks and followed Sue to the "Hen do proper."

I was surprised to see, as we turned the corner, we were going into the rabbit bar – Jane and I called it that because there was always a six-foot rabbit outside and I still can't remember to this day what it is called but it was at the traffic lights opposite the Grand for anyone that gives a shit. In fact, I think it was called Harveys though what that has to do with a giant rabbit I do not know.

We went inside and were pleasantly surprised that it was like it always was, a nice and quite trendy bar and not an inflatable cock in sight.

Alas, I was wrong, for a split second I thought this was it but no, this is Sue we are talking about and she strutted through the bar shouting various obscenities to perplexed looking bar staff until she found "the brother"

Haaaa! He was a cross between the Fonz from Happy Days and Tubbs and Crocket from Miami Vice.

"Follow me ladies to the pleasure dome" said the fonz, what a prick, I thought.

Throw a bit of Frankie goes to Hollywood in for good measure to that description!

We arrived at "The Pleasure Dome" to be greeted by semi naked men with glasses of shots in their hand, a room full of balloons, very loud music, very dark and very smoky.

Sue shouted above the music "Come on ladies, take your pick, the more you drink the more they strip"

Oh, for fucks sake this I cannot take, Mum and Marie had had a couple of glasses of wine already and were loosening up too much for my liking, this was only going to end horrendously, I could just tell.

The night progressed, and Sue was in fact totally correct, she had downed a full tray of shots and the semi naked man was now stood with an empty tray, a smile on his face and not much else.

Is this even legal to have naked men in a licenced establishment? I thought.

After dancing to the whole back catalogue of Stock Aitken and Waterman I went to the bar to get a drink. As I waited to be served I looked over to the ladies to see that Sue was now getting more objects out of her carrier bag, Jesus it was like Mary Poppins bag.

The music suddenly dropped 10 decibels and you could now hear yourself think at least.

"Time for games" screamed Sue.

Nice!!!!! Can't wait, I thought.

She produced a various array of phallic looking objects of all shapes, sizes and colours and set them out at the other end of the room.

Naked Frank was back with another tray of shots but thank god he had now put his pants on, I think that was down to Sue, as she and Frank disappeared for a while, so I'm guessing he is now off limits! My heart bleeds.

So, the object of the game was to down a shot and run to the other side of the room and grab the "Object" that was most like your partners.

I for one would NOT be looking to see what Marie or my mother picked out, that, I DID NOT NEED TO SEE OR KNOW.

We then did the same but had to pick what we most wanted, then least wanted and so on and so on.

This lasted quite a while and to end it all we were all given a chocolate Penis!

The music was back on, the drinks were flowing, and I was just hoping it was nearly time to go home.

I happened to look over to where my Mum and Marie were sat to find them both with a semi naked man stretched out over both of them and they were hysterically laughing at whatever it was he was telling them, and they were both sucking on a chocolate penis.

"Time to go Jane" I shouted as I nodded over to the mothers.

We said our thanks and goodbyes to everyone and dragged the mothers out, as we got outside and turned the corner we went down to the taxi rank. Jane happened to say, "Do you fancy a kebab while we wait for the taxi."

Before I could get my words out, both mothers were shouting "Kebab, Kebab" or even babbab at one point.

So here we were, in the Alternative Two, ordering kebabs with our mothers!!! I never thought I would see the day.

The journey home was quiet, the kebab must have sobered them up.

At last I was home, the last to be dropped off and ready for my bed but no, they had all got out and not one of them had thought about paying!!!

"Erm if you can drop me here I can run inside and get some money" I said deeply embarrassed that I didn't have enough money on me and hoping to god Carl was in and had some.

"I don't think so love, I know your game you are going to do a runner, leave your bag and you can go get the money" spat the taxi man.

Jesus what do I look like, a criminal? I have never run away from a taxi, oh shit wait a minute, ok well maybe just the once!

I ran inside and woke Carl up, he sorted the taxi man, got my bag and sent him on his way.

"So how was it" enquired Carl.

I told him it all from start to finish, he was beside himself laughing and I just knew he would use this as ammunition should the need ever occur.

With that we went to bed knowing that we had the packing to do in the morning and a trip to see Bob.

Chapter 18

I felt ok the day after but thought I would ring Janes house to check she was ok. All good there and Dave had said how surprised he was he didn't have to carry her out of the taxi or pay a fine for her throwing up in the back of it! He was impressed, maybe we were growing up.

I rang my Mum, well I say my Mum, but I couldn't talk to her as she was still in bed. My Dad was talking in hushed tones and couldn't quite get all his words out without laughing.

"Oh, Clare you should have seen the state of her, well I'm sure you did" said Dad.

"She didn't seem that bad after her Kebab" I said.

"I think it was the kebab or babbab as she insisted on calling it that tipped her over the edge" said Dad.

He explained she didn't seem too bad walking down the drive but as soon as she got inside, she was singing and dancing and telling him she had had the best night ever, she had never seen as many willys in her life and did you know you could get chocolate ones!

She then explained about the babbab and how the lovely young Asian man had said you have to have extra chilli sauce for the taste and how lovely it was and then he said she went very quiet, very pale and stumbled upstairs, to the bathroom and she stayed there for about an hour, talking to Hughie.

She was still in bed and he didn't think she would be making an appearance anytime soon.

I asked Dad if he wanted to join us at Bobs, but he declined saying he had better stay here to keep an eye on the babbab queen. We both laughed.

I had no sooner put the phone down when it rang again, it was James my brother in Law.

"Thank god for that, I've been trying you and your Mum and Dad for ages and couldn't get through" said James.

I was just about to explain what happened when he said we are at the hospital, everything is ok, and I think you are going to be an auntie very soon and can I let my parents know. I wished them all good luck, said I loved them all and asked him to phone my parents when there was any news as we would go over there now.

I put the phone down and told Carl we needed to get to my parents.

I burst through the door and explained everything to my Dad. I then ran upstairs to find the kebab queen was getting out of bed, she had obviously heard the commotion and was getting up.

The shock of being a Grandma anytime soon was enough for our Margo, to sober her up. She was washed, dressed and downstairs getting a plan sorted before you could say "Do you fancy another shot mother."

She had the coffee brewing (yes of course they had the coffee machine I wanted, that goes without saying) The bacon cooking (how on earth she did that, I didn't have half as much as her to drink last night and the smell was turning my stomach).

My Dad was pacing up and down, my Mum was making 364 bacon sarnies and Carl and I were just sat watching them both and realising what a momentous occasion this was, waiting for the news of the birth of their first grandchild. Very exciting and I did chuckle thinking I bet my sister is in absolute agony now, it's a sibling thing!

So, we sat, and we sat, and we jumped every time the phone rang. Dad was sent to go get my Grandma, she had to be included in all this sitting about and then it finally happened.

James called to tell us there was no news yet, but he didn't think it would be long.

For fucks sake man don't do that to us, don't call to tell us there is no news, my nerves can't take it!!!!

I bet he had no sooner got back to my sister when the inevitable happened as he called us back 20 minutes later to welcome my beautiful niece to the world.

Yes, you have it folks Louisa Jane was born at 17.22pm today weighing 7lbs and 4oz's

Mum, Dad and Grandma were ready with their coats on to go down, I said Carl and I would wait until tomorrow, not that I wasn't dying to see them, but I thought it was a day for grandparents and great grandparents.

We saw them go and part of me wished it was me they were going to see that I had just given birth and then reality hit, and I thought I was being silly, so we set off to see Bob. I hope he had saved some tea for us!

I needn't have worried, Bob was very practical and once we had told him our news and that we weren't sure what time we would be with him he decided on a salad, so it wouldn't spoil. And a lovely salad it was too.

We stayed with Bob for quite a while and I told him all about last night and the birth of my niece and we played with Scamp, who by now was growing quite a bit but still very puppy like and sooooooooooo cute!

Carl and he got on to talking about the business, so I took Scamp for a walk, it was lovely to be alone having spent what felt like days held hostage at my Mums.

It gave me time to think about the recent events and that today was the birth of my parents first grandchild, my sister was a Mummy, it was a massive bloody deal and things were changing so much. We were all growing up and getting more responsibilities, we were getting sensible and I wasn't sure about it. I had bought a house! That was massive, what a responsibility but not quite as massive as having a baby so that put me straight.

By the time I got back to the house Carl and Bob seemed to be celebrating. Oh, that's sweet toasting the baby's head but I guess I am driving home!

As I got nearer I noticed some official looking documents on the coffee table and as I walked in, Carl stood up, picked up the documents and said, "Bob has made me a partner in his business, I have 45% shares."

"Whaaaat? Eh?" I didn't understand at all.

Bob explained that as he didn't have any children and he thought of us as his children it was the right thing to do.

This way he could teach Carl every aspect of the business, in the hope that one day it would all be his and he could carry on the business.

"But you have already given us so much Bob we can't accept this" I said.

But he wasn't having any of it and insisted it was what he wanted to do, he wanted the business to go on long after he had gone, and Carl could do that and pass it on to his sons or daughters.

He didn't have any family and it was something he had thought about long and hard and he knew June would approve.

I was so touched and so grateful, Bob was one in a million and I loved him like a Grandad though I am not sure if technically that was possible, but I wasn't going to argue.

Bob and Carl carried on talking business and what they were and weren't going to do with it to grow it. Carl had learnt a lot at college (Uni sorry) and couldn't wait to put some of it into practise.

Bob trusted him with his life and so did I, he really was the most amazing person and I couldn't wait to be his wife and the mother to his children. Things were certainly on the up for us and the sky was the limit.

Chapter 19

The wedding eve had arrived, I had just got back from work, no sign of Carl but then I didn't expect to see him, as he was working longer hours now.

I packed my overnight bag, grabbed my wedding things for the day after, the majority of which were already at Marie's, as she had insisted the bridesmaid's dresses were taken straight to her house for safe keeping.

I was calling in to see my sister at home first and Louisa, who I have to say is the most gorgeous baby I have ever seen, Carl and I are totally besotted, in fact we all are, and Mum and baby are doing great.

I eventually got to Marie's as I couldn't tear myself away from Louisa and her tiny fingers and that amazing new baby smell, a bit like a new car smell really, one of those smells you can't beat.

I digress sorry, so I got to Marie's eventually and I think world war 3 had broken out. Marie was in tears, Jane was acting like a petulant child and Mark was just chilling with a fag and a cuppa.

"Give us a fag Mark" I said pointing at the kettle at the same time.

We sat for a bit enjoying our brew and fag with Mark telling me that Marie and Jane had started arguing over the time the hairdresser was coming in the morning. Marie has her coming at sparrows fart and Jane thinks it's too early.

"It's no big deal, for a start she will be late and then she will sit and have a fag and a cuppa. Marie will be pleased she's here and Jane will be pleased she's not doing her stuff straight away" said Mark really not that bothered.

He was right, and I get the tension, it is a big thing and Jane and Marie can bicker at the slightest thing normally, so the eve of the wedding was never going to be any different.

I plucked up courage to go join them and suggested Jane and I go for a walk, mainly to go get some fags but I lied and said we would go for a walk and pretend we were 16 again and reflect on what was about to happen tomorrow.

Marie loved the idea and thought it was very poignant that I would think of such a lovely thing. Yes, ok Marie, we need fags if we are spending the night here! I might even throw in a cheeky bottle of wine, well it's the eve of the wedding after all.

I don't know what it is but as soon as Jane and I are back at her parents I do feel 16 again and to be fair Marie does treat us as that age when we are there so let's not let her down.

We snook in with some fags, sweets and wine and ran upstairs to get the party started. Jane put Mel and Kim on "Respectable" that was our TUNE as we modelled ourselves on them, back in the day and we swigged the wine from the bottle that had dutifully been opened by the corkscrew still hidden in a drawer in Janes old bedroom.

We did our dance routine to it, lit a fag and fell back on the bed laughing.

We reminisced for quite a while about the good old days and how weird was it that tomorrow Jane would become a Mrs, and all grown up and that I had bought a house and had shares in a company and soon to be married myself.

We had both come a long way and this was just the start of more exciting things, but first things first, let's go taunt Marie a bit, well it would be rude not to.

"Mum, do you want me to set the table" asked Jane.

"Oh yes please love, dinner will be about 20 minutes" replied Marie.

"Fork and Knife Mum? Fork and Knife?" said Jane repeatedly to which I was creased over because I knew what was coming.

"What fork and knife are you talking about "screeched Marie.

To which we fell about, and Jane replied, "No need to swear mother."

It got her every time and made us howl with laughter, very childish I know, but very funny. Try it.

"Grow up you two, you are acting like children" said Marie with a little twinkle in her eye, she loved it really.

We all sat down to dinner, that was a full roast dinner and Marie was cracking at roast dinners and she served her Yorkshire puddings with the main meal and always did garlic mushrooms to start.

Delicious, ooh and Janes Grandma joined us, much to the dismay of Marie, as it was Marks Mum, she was hilarious, and we called her Grandma Chuff as everything was chuffing this and chuffing that, she was hilarious and I'm sure she did it to wind Marie up.

We finished dinner and Marie announced, "Do you want to get your mother home Mark, so she can get ready for tomorrow" a polite way of saying "get this woman out of here now."

"Oh, don't mind me Marie, I just need a bit of a chuffing cat lick in the morning and I'll be ready" said Grandma chuff with a wink to us girls and off she went out of the house and up the path farting as she went.

Whilst Mark was taking his Mum home and Marie was clearing the dinner things we thought we would try out Janes wedding make up and I said I would do it for her.

We ran upstairs, had a fag obviously and then I started, at first being quite good then got bored and put bright pink blusher on Janes eyes coming out to a point and going straight into a thick line of bright pink blusher down her cheeks. Topped off with electric blue eyeliner, a bit of coral lipstick and to top it off Coca Cola flavoured lip gloss, you know the ones with the ball at the end that you could bite out. It must have been hidden for god knows how many years in Janes make up bag.

"Ta dah, all ready, now don't peak but go show your Mum your wedding make up, she will love the subtlety of it" I lied and couldn't believe Jane fell for it.

We ran downstairs. "What the hell, over my dead body are you wearing that amount of make-up, oh for god's sake what have you done" cried Marie getting all worked up again.

Jane looked over in the mirror and howled laughing "don't you like it Mum, its soooooooooo this year and I think the bridesmaids will be the same."

On realising it was a wind-up. Marie laughed and said how we would never grow up and bugger off upstairs, she needed a stiff drink.

Yes, ok Marie, to go with the bottle you had downed whilst making tea, I thought.

We obliged, cracked open the wine again and decided we would have a bath and get our jarmies on.

Jane laid in the bath and I was sat on the loo reading out her horoscope from the Jackie magazine Marie still insisted on buying when we were both round at her house. Although I am pretty sure this was an old one as Wham were on the front cover advertising Last Christmas!

As I was not the bride and not considered as important, I had to get the bath second and could only top the water up not run a new one. "It's expensive you know, and you will realise when you get a place of your own" Marie had said on numerous occasions over the years.

We eventually went back downstairs, and Mark was back, having safely delivered farting Grandma chuff home.

We all sat chatting and having a cuppa for quite a while when we realised just how late it was and all decided to retire to Bedfordshire – one of Marks sayings!

The morning of the wedding had finally arrived, and Jane needn't be worried about the time the hairdresser was coming, she was late, Marie was flapping but Jane was secretly quite pleased.

Mark and I were in the garden having a cuppa and a fag when she finally arrived, flapping as usual and rushing passed us to get into the bride.

Mark and I stayed there for a while and I think Mark was quite emotional that morning but like I have mentioned before it's a big day when your daughter gets married whether they are still at home or not.

The hair went well, surprisingly, and the flowers arrived on time and Jane was now doing her make up just as the photographer arrived to take the "bride getting ready shots."

Shit, I had better make myself half decent just in case he wanted me in any of them, so off I dashed to get ready.

We were all done and dusted in no time and managed to get some nice photos of us all, then Mark said the dreaded words that Marie really didn't want to hear "Right love, I'll just go and get my mother."

That's all we needed, farting chuffer to lower the tone somewhat.

By the time the fartinator had arrived, looking all pretty in her two piece and fascinator, which looked like she had a shuttlecock on her head, we were all ready and Jane had her dress on but was upstairs still waiting for her Dad to see her.

"So where is she then the virginal chuffing bride" said the great chuffer herself.

"She's upstairs Grandma, waiting for Mark to go up and see her" I said trying to be all lovely to the old dear.

"What for, he can't tell her owt she doesn't already chuffing know now, in fact she can probably teach him a thing or two, you young uns now with your chuffing alcho pops and your chuffing drugs I don't know" chuffed Grandma and on and on she went.

"I think it is more that she wants her Dad to see her in her dress before anyone else more than anything" I said losing patience and not really giving a shit, so I went back outside for a fag to find Marie sat at the bottom of the garden and was I correct in what I saw, she was having a sneaky fag!!!!

"Erm what do you think you are doing" I laughed to her.

"Don't say a word, I just fancied one, what with the wedding and his bloody mother huffing and chuffing, I couldn't help it" said Marie and we both laughed and sat for the rest of our smoke break in silence.

Mark appeared a little later and looked quite teary eyed, I was guessing he had seen Jane in her dress.

"Marie Love, our Jane is ready to come down if you two can help her and by god she looks bloody gorgeous" said the proud Dad.

Marie and I went upstairs and into Marie's bedroom where Jane was stood in all her finery looking gorgeous.

Over the cries of "you look stunning and how gorgeous the dress was" and "your hair is amazing" etc we could hear

Grandma chuff shouting "Stop pissing about you lot the chuffing cars are here."

Where did time go?? We were ready for the off. Jane and her Dad were going in the Rolls Royce and me, Marie and Grandma chuff were in a white Mercedes Benz.

We were going first, straight to the church and meeting the other bridesmaids and page boys there, they were only little, so we thought it would be best for them to go with their parents then we didn't have to deal with the brats at all.

"Right mate well here's to it, you look bloody ace, I love you to bits, enjoy every second of the day and I'll see you at church" I said, just as we both started blubbing, then laughing because we were crying and off I went to get Grandma chuff in the car. I needn't have bothered she was already in the front seat.

"Come on, chuffing hell where's bloody Marie now? we will be late you know, it's only the bride that is meant to be late not us chuffers" she tutted, and I just caught sight of the chauffeur's face as she started on her rampage, I gave him a little wink and smile, and I think he got the message.

Finally, we were off and within a few minutes we were pulling up at St Margaret's Church in Horsforth, it was a beautiful church and I got christened there, not that I can remember, obviously.

The little bridesmaids were there already all hyper and annoying and the two-page boys, Janes cousin's children, were both crying and hating the attention already.

I spotted Carl straight away, he came over, gave me a kiss and told me I looked gorgeous and went and did the same to Marie and Chuffer.

He had waited outside to see us before he went to take his place with Dave inside. This was his cue to go as he knew Jane and Mark wouldn't be long and with that he gave me a wink and went inside.

I was beginning to feel nervous, so I rounded the bridesmaids up, told everyone to go inside and it just left Marie and me. Marie was meant to be in the church already, but she wouldn't go in until Jane had arrived. We saw the car pull up to which the twats oops I mean the beautiful little bridesmaids screamed, which frightened me to death.

Marie ran over, gave her daughter a kiss and nearly ran inside singing, "It's time, its time!"

Jane and Mark had a couple of photos getting out of the car and then it was time. We were walking behind them, down the aisle and god it was a long one, the music started and off we went. Me trying to smile whilst keeping the little bastards in line.

Just as were about to go in, I grabbed the bridesmaids, smiled sweetly and told them if they behaved all the way now and through the service I will give them a pound each and some sweets and I will tell their parents how good they have been. They got my look and my message, and I have to say they were little angels, that and I held their hands very tightly throughout the service, very tightly!

It was perfect and went so quickly and before I knew it, it was time to walk back down the aisle only this time I was walking back with the best man, my Carl and he looked bloody gorgeous in his morning suit.

Now was the time to party and go to the hotel for the best bit of any wedding. They had their reception at the Norfolk Gardens and I have to say it was lovely and the staff were amazing and very attentive.

We lined up to meet all the guests and to be fair I knew most them and it was nice to see some I hadn't seen in years.

Jane had decided to have the speeches first as she knew Dave, Carl and her Dad were quite nervous, and she wanted them to enjoy their meal and not have to worry as it would all be done and dusted by then. It was a really good idea and one I had mentally noted, that and not to have little bastards, oops I mean little Bridesmaids.

The speeches were fantastic, and Mark had us all crying with stories of Jane when she was little.

Dave's was very romantic and said how lucky he was to be marrying his best friend and Carl's, well it had us all in stitches about how he and Dave first met, how they both fancied us both back in school and how cool Dave was and how he was a bit backward in coming forward and the stuff the four of us had got up to and what there was to come.

He finished off by saying "here's a toast to a perfect couple and ones I think of as my family and let's raise a glass to the bride and groom." I was in bits, it was perfect, and it had given me the wedding bug.

The meal was simple but lovely, yet another roast dinner but not a Yorkshire in sight not as a starter or with the main. It was soup to start, chicken dinner and trifle. Very simple but you can't go too fancy when you are catering for so many people.

The tables were adorned with flower petals, nice touch, but I was thinking more diamonds for mine or maybe both and we all received a bride's favour with the obligatory sugar almonds. Now god forbid I am turning into my mother but each one had about ten in and I am sure there is only meant to be five and each of them stand for something like love, honour, trust etc etc so that's something else noted that I will do correctly, just saying.

So that was that and it was now time to go back to our hotel room, as most of the wedding party were staying over. The hotel staff could get the room ready for the night do. All the gifts had been taken to the honeymoon suite and just as we were leaving Dave grabbed my arm, told me their room number and said to meet him and Jane there with Carl.

So, we did and as we got there they had got a bottle of champagne for all four of us to enjoy without any of the other guests.

The room was amazing and more like a suite with a separate sitting area. Lovely, but I wouldn't be getting married here, we can't have the same reception venue now can we.

We stayed with them a good hour and still had nearly two hours to kill, so off we went to our room to have a little lie down and refresh ourselves for the evening's festivities.

We must have fallen asleep because I woke with a start and realised it was half seven and the party started at half seven.

We quickly dressed, tidied ourselves up and went to join the others. The room had transformed completely as all the tables were now smaller and positioned around a dance floor and the disco had started.

Phew, we were just in time for the first dance and the song of their choice was "Whitney Houston's, I will always love you."

They looked so in love as they danced, and I have never seen either of them look happier, they then motioned for us all to join in and it was perfect.

The rest of the night went off without a hitch, we danced and drank and laughed and danced some more, to all our old favourites, in fact at one point all four of us were at different parts of the room and a Smiths song came on and we all ran to get to the dance floor. We loved a bit of Morrisey.

All in all, it was a perfect wedding and they were a perfect couple, heading off the day after to Turkey for their honeymoon and me and Carl would be packing as we move into our new home in just a week.

Chapter 20

So far so good. We got the keys the week before, so we could get it decorated, just magnolia in every room to freshen it up, so we just looked around and it looked so much bigger now there was no furniture in.

Ooh I was going to like shopping for the new furniture, but first we had to get all our stuff over there, which to be fair didn't take long as moving from a one bedroom flat you didn't have a lot to move.

The main thing was curtains, now I am my mother's daughter, so I had arranged for them to be fitted today, well the lounge, dining room and our bedroom all the others were off the peg and would be put up by myself.

The carpets were ok, so they had been professionally cleaned, my Mum insisted so she arranged and paid for that.

By lunchtime it was beginning to look like a home, even more so once I unpacked my spanking new state of the art coffee machine complete with milk steamer wand, which pissed my Mum off no end as ours was better than hers! Should have waited Margo and not been so keen to get one.

We got fish and chips from Slaters on New Road Side, and they were delicious. We met a couple of the neighbours, an old couple to one side, he was a retired headmaster and his wife and a young couple adjoining us with a small baby, a bit older than us I would say.

It was a very quiet street and had very well looked after gardens, thank god my Dad was keen as I couldn't let the street down.

Curtains all up, bed in place, coffee machine working, and in pride of place doll's house of our Forever Home. It looked perfect in the dining room, in the little alcove at the side of the fire and the drawings of the house were up on the chimney breast.

It looked fab and I couldn't wait for Jane and Dave to get back to show them. They still had a week left of their honeymoon, but we had received a postcard from them, in fact it was the first piece of post we got, and they must have literally posted it as they landed.

It just read:

Hotel Fab, Weather hot,
Beer Cheap, Dave has shits already
Wish you were here!
xxx

What more could we wish for, at least they were having fun.

So, as we said goodbye that night and thankyou to all our helpers we realised it was finally here, we had finally moved in to our new home and we loved it already.

Bob had brought us a plant for the garden, a white rose bush which my Dad thought was amazing, and my sister brought a framed photo of my niece and some flowers and my Mum and Dad said they would buy us a dining room set as they said what's the point in having a dining room if you can't use it and my Grandma gave us money to put towards something we really wanted.

I would say we were nearly there, it did look fantastic and I couldn't wait to start our new life here!

I had booked a couple of days off work following the move, so I could get things just right and of course I planned to get a dining room set as soon as my Mum was free. We had looked all over and finally decided on a pine table and chairs. Yes, I did say we decided and I didn't mean me and Carl, because my Mum and Dad were buying it then my Mum had to like it!!

I had made one of my famous lists and so far, to get the house just perfect was:
Dining table and chairs
Chair for side of fire in dining room
New Kitchen and extension
Telephone table and seat
Coat stand
New settee and
Coffee table and rug as Mum's old rug we had was now soooooooooo last year.
Two spare double beds
Laundry basket – nice one to match the bathroom
So really there wasn't that much to buy or do. Everywhere was painted, the carpets had all been cleaned and I would eventually like a wooden floor in the hallway, I think it makes a place look very classy.

All I had to do now was rustle something up for tea as Bob was coming and bringing Scamp to show him our new home.

Chapter 21

So, Jane and Dave were due back from their honeymoon, we had moved in and got everything sorted and I was back at work doing everyone's head in now about my new house. Derek was loving it!!!

I suddenly felt all grown up taking about "My House" it was different when we had a flat, that felt quite childlike, almost like we were playing at being grownups, but this felt different and I was proud of us. Oh, and very grateful to Bob and our parents.

Work was quiet today for some reason, I don't mean there was no work in just that there was hushed voices and office doors closed and a lot of new faces milling about, One, a tall bloke, quite old but very distinguished looking.

"Cop a load of that" said Jennie, one of my colleagues, "I wouldn't kick him out of bed for farting" she continued, we howled with laughter only to realise he might have heard,

"I am so glad I didn't say that I would have died" I said still laughing.

We kept seeing him going up and down the office and decided he must fancy one of us as he kept staring as he walked past.

"Hey, it might be me, they do say once you have a ring on your finger you become so much more attractive to the opposite sex" I said still laughing and I hadn't even got the words out of my mouth when he came over and looking me straight in the eye said "Clare, do you have a minute please, if you could follow me".

Oh fuck, I thought, I've done it now!

I followed him down the office and I could see everyone staring as I walked past.

We got to the MD's office and as he walked in he motioned for me to sit at the chair at the near side of the desk. I noticed immediately that there was a woman sat in the corner of the room, I had no idea who she was, but I nearly shit myself when I saw her and if I hadn't been so nervous I would have probably said that.

"Ok Clare, now before we start, can Mandy get you a coffee?" He pointed over to the bitch in the corner that gave me the fright of my life.

"Yes, please Mandy" I said, looking straight at her, "Coffee please, white one sugar" I said thinking yes, you cow you scared me so make my coffee bitch.

Off she went, and nameless hot guy continued.

"You have nothing to worry about, you are not here to be chastised, you haven't done anything wrong, but I think I must first make some introductions. I am Daniel Craig." (Before you say it, it was way, way, before James Bond so no I didn't just nick the name because I couldn't be arsed thinking up a new one.)

"I am the owner of this company, now you won't necessarily have heard of me as I was, up until recently, a silent partner, I have however, now bought out the whole business and will be looking at setting up a new office in Leeds City Centre. I will be specialising in high end corporate clients."

"I will be leaving this branch to run, very successfully as it is, but it isn't my thing, it concentrates more on local people and local businesses. So as my specialism is large blue-chip companies I decided we needed blue chip offices in the centre of Leeds."

Mandy had now returned with my coffee and I thanked her and got a little cocky as I knew now I wasn't in trouble.

"Do carry on Daniel" I said quite smugly and probably a little cocky, but after all this talk of blue chips and high ends I felt very grown up. I had no idea what it all meant but none the less, I felt grown up and to be fair Mandy looked a bit thick, very young, (says me Mrs mature now) and she was probably just there to make the coffee.

"This is Mandy Mitchell and she is overseeing the new proposition, she is my Secretary, but she is helping me to make sure we get the correct staff for our new office and we are looking at taking the crème de la crème from here and then recruiting any other staff we may need externally" said DC.

Well that told me, she wasn't thick or a coffee maker after all. I like Mandy, I bet she is a real laugh on a night out!

"So, what do you want me to do?" I said as I really was very confused now.

"Well, Mandy and I have been keeping a close eye on you lot for quite a while, looking at time keeping and mainly concentrating on everyone's appraisals and I have to say you stood out. From starting with the company, you have progressed quite quickly, and you seem to be a very valued member of the team and because of that I would like to ask you to join us at our new offices and be assistant Manager to your current Manager who will also be joining us" said DC.

I didn't know what to say, I asked who else was going and he said we all had to keep it very quiet for the time being as they were getting everyone in and telling them the news about the new office.

Some would be asked to join them, like me, and some would be staying here. It wasn't a blight on them, it was just they were basically picking who they wanted but it had to be kept a secret until everyone that had been asked to move had signed their new contract with their new terms and conditions.

I didn't understand why anyone wouldn't want to move so I asked DC.

"Some people took a job here as its near to home, local, they know most of their clients and basically its handy for them and they don't mind ticking over here, you on the other hand look like a young woman with ambition and won't mind the drive to Leeds every day and will look forward to the challenge"

"I see, you also mentioned a new contract" I said.

With that, DC (Can't be arsed with full names all the time) motioned over to Mandy (MY New BFF) and she handed him my contract, who then in turn handed it to me.

"If you want to take some time to read and digest this then please feel free" said DC.

I think I did, so I sat, and I turned the first page, Jesus H, the salary was pretty good, free parking, company pension, Gym Membership (you can stick that right up your arse) 9 to 5 every day, 22 days holiday, bank holiday and a bonus scheme and shares.

"That all seems pretty good to me, where do I sign?" I said looking at both Mand and DC.

"You can take longer if you like, don't feel pressured, take it home to show your husband if you like" said Mandy.

"Fiancée, we aren't married yet, but we have just moved into a beautiful new house and no thank you I will sign now, my Dad always says if it feels right then it is right and quite honestly what have I got to lose. I will be on more money, working in the centre of Leeds and I have been promoted, sign me up Mandy" I said, probably a little smug but Mandy did smile as I said it.

Daniel promptly jumped up and shook my hand and said, "Welcome on-board Clare and may we all sail away to the promised land together."

Steady on DC you are beginning to sound like a right twat and I did think you were OK.

I finished my coffee, while telling them all about my new house and new niece and how my best friend had just got married and my fiancé was a partner in a large and very successful building firm. They seemed to enjoy the one-way conversation. I left the office and as I did my Manager nodded to me to go to the kitchen straight away.

"Quick question so as not to arouse suspicion, did you say yes or no?" she said in a very hushed and rushed voice.

"Yes" I said and with that she gave me the thumbs up and was gone. Well I might as well have a fag and coffee now I'm in the kitchen.

A few of the other girls rushed in asking what it was about, and I said it's a new manager and he is introducing himself to everyone, nothing to worry about and it wasn't a lie, there was nothing for any of them to worry about.

The next few days were tough, now I knew what they were going in the office for I was trying to read their faces when they came out. The ones that were smiling had obviously been asked to move and the ones that didn't look any different didn't know any different, so they were staying.

If I had read them right I was pleased with the outcome of the ones they had chosen but we would find out tomorrow who was in and who was out.

I had explained everything to Carl, obviously, and he seemed proud that I had made my mind up on the spot and like he said, it didn't matter who was going and who will be staying, if I was happy with what I was doing, no one else really matters and he was right, he was always right.

Friday was here, and I saw DC come out of the office with little Mandy trotting behind him. He made a little speech and informed every one of the move and that our office had been found and we would be moving in a couple of weeks.

Shit that quick, I thought it would be months.

He also said a few of the current staff would be moving and if we could raise our hands now, those of us who would be moving. I really don't think that was the correct way to go about it but hey ho, it was what it was. As I put my hand up I was looking round to see who else was coming and I was spot on with my predictions.

Accounts would still be based here in Stanningley and they would be getting a new assistant for the extra work so accounts were pleased, it made sense for the standard general team to stay as they knew their local clients and all lived locally so he got round it like that, maybe he was bullshitting me saying they want the crème de la crème but who gives a shit, I'm working in town, with all the shops at lunchtime which will beat Hardacres on a lunchtime, no offence but you can't spend an hour in there choosing a butty and a bun.

So, it was set and all out in the open. Phew.

Chapter 22

We were at Mums for tea a few weeks after and so was Lilly and James and Louisa, she was growing so fast and so beautiful I loved her so much and thought she was the prettiest baby around.

We were sat discussing Louisa's christening when my sister asked Carl and I if we would be God Parents, we were thrilled, and I cried, to which my sister took the piss for the rest of the night.

This year has seen me be a bridesmaid, a homeowner and now a God Parent! How very bloody exciting.

The christening was only a few weeks away and thank god I didn't have anything to do, other than to get new outfits for me and Carl and a beautiful gift for our God Daughter and I knew just the gift.

I discussed the complexity of it with Bob, I didn't want to bother Carl - and Bob said he would do it no problem.

You see basically, I asked Bob to build "My Forever House" not as a doll's house, that had been done, but as a play house and I thought if we kept it at my parents then my children could also play in it and it would be part of us all then. Touching eh?? I thought so too.

The arrangements for the Christening were going very well, well I think they were, but I wasn't involved so I had no stress or care really.

Bob rang me a few weeks after our initial discussion about the gift for my God Daughter and said it was ready and he was taking it round to my parents' house, they were in on it and thought it was a beautiful idea.

I drove over to Mum and Dads to find Bob putting the last bit in place. Oh my god it looked amazing, obviously it wasn't the same, but you got the idea and all I had to do was put up some curtains and get some plants for the porch.

It was perfect, and I am sure when Louisa is a bit older she will spend hours in there and hopefully with her cousins too!

The Christening saw us back at St Margaret's, only this time we were here to celebrate the christening of our beautiful niece and Goddaughter Louisa.

Carl and I were at the front with the proud parents, Christine, Lilly's friend from school (the other godmother) and the star of the show Louisa looking as beautiful as ever in her christening gown - the very same one worn by my sister and I, my Mum and my Uncle and Grandma, so it was very traditional and very bloody old.

The service was beautiful and concentrated on the love we are to show Louisa and support, as she goes through life.

Jane and Dave were there, obviously and so was Bob. He was looking happier now Carl had taken on more responsibility and he was doing less hours.

The service was over and back to Mum and Dads for afternoon tea and she had done it all herself, well she had caterers in, but she had arranged it all herself and she would be making the tea and coffee, not a waiter in site!

To be honest I think my Dad put his foot down on this one, after all, they had a wedding to pay for and it wasn't going to be long.

It was a beautiful sunny day and most us were outside, various people were admiring the Wendy House and I had to tell them the story of it and explain how it came to be.

I saw Jane and Dave over in the corner of the garden and manged to weave my way through to get to them. We hadn't seen much of them since they got back from their honeymoon as they were now looking to move to a new house and Carl was so busy at work and I was quite happy in my new home making it all homey and beautiful.

"Hi, you two, how are you both" I said and gave them both a kiss.

They smirked and gave each other a knowing look and simply replied they were both ok. I knew something was going on but couldn't quite put my finger on it. We chatted for a while and it wasn't until we went into Mums dining room and we were tucking into the buffet when Dave said to Jane "You can't have prawns love, remember" and he took the spoon off her.

"Oh my god, you are preggers" I whispered to Jane.
"Sssssssh we don't want to make a fuss, not today it wouldn't be fair, but yes we are" exclaimed Jane.

"Now hang on there just one moment mate, I am bloody thrilled for you both but drop the WE are preggers, you are my dear, not Dave, he had made it happen yes and is 50% of this baby but NO NO NO he is NOT and never will be PREGGERS ". I laughed and hugged her.

She was still laughing when my Mum came up and just quietly said "If I didn't know you better Jane, I would swear you were blooming." with that she winked and went back to the kitchen.

Steady on now Margo and mother of all mothers, don't pretend to us you didn't just hear our conversation. She had a wonderful knack of doing that, my old Mum, she would earwig, hear something and then say, "If I didn't know better" and all that bollocks, she was a nosey cow, but we loved her.

"Can I tell Carl? "I whispered to Jane

"Like you wouldn't anyway, you tell him everything, but we had actually planned to come over to yours and tell you both together" said Jane.

"So is that a yes or a no "I enquired.

"For fucks sake tell him "Jane laughed.

I caught Carl's eye and signalled for him to come over and join us. He had no sooner got to us when Dave told him, I think he wanted to get in there before me and to be honest I don't blame him because I was just about to open my mouth and tell him and it wasn't really my thing to tell was it.

We were thrilled for them, even though, yet again, a part of me was jealous, again, I would get over it. It was all happening.

We then realised that Jane would be heavily pregnant for my wedding, oops had I not mentioned that we get married in 4 months' time, so sorry but with everything going on I must have forgotten.

Yes, we were getting married in August and everything was sorted and booked, the dress purchased, bridesmaids sorted. Only now we would have to get one altered!!!

The plans all went without a hitch really, we had already decided when, where and how.

Obviously, it would be St Margaret's Church and the reception had been arranged at one of our favourite restaurants.

Both our parents had said who they thought should be bridesmaids and page boys and we took all that into consideration and did our own thing. Well it was "Our Day."

Flowers and car sorted and everything else that needed doing had been.

Don't forget but I had been planning this for years, isn't that what every little girl does?

Chapter 23

By now I had moved into my new office at work and god was it posh, very sleek and very high end and I loved it. I could see me being here forever and DC was great to work for, very encouraging and taking me out of my comfort zone to grow me and show me that reaching forward was the only way to go.

Mandy was ok too to be fair, she was very quiet, very clever and quite plain really, the total opposite of me but we got on and occasionally had a quick drink after work Well I had nothing to rush home for, Carl was working more and more hours which was great, and the money was fantastic, we had it stashed all over the house. You see rule one of being a builder was to do some jobs cash in hand and keep that money in a safe in your house. That was Bobs thinking and Carl was doing just as he was told.

We did have a safe fitted and I have no idea how much is in there, but Carl is always putting money in, it just didn't really interest me that much and if I wanted to know I only had to ask.

So, work was good for me and Carl but like I said he was working some stupid hours and working away a few nights. The reasoning behind all this was one of his builder mates had moved to Derby and got a job with a local builder but he said it was crap but the lads he worked with were really decent so Carl and Bob decided to branch out and opened up in Derby using these lads and it was going great as far as I knew but it did mean Carl was spending a lot of time there to get it all up and running.

If he wasn't working, he was at home doing the books and putting money in the safe. I told him he needed some help with the accounts side and I volunteered my Mum, she was good with this sort of thing, very organised and had held numerous high-powered positions in her career and it would get her out from under my Dad's feet.

So that was settled, Carl dropped all the stuff at her house and off she went.

I was hoping this would free up his time and we would be able to plan a few breaks away but alas no, we had the wedding coming up and no time for that.

We went over to Jane and Dave's for tea one night which was a lovely change, she was showing quite a bit and I asked Dave when he was getting his empathy belly, after all they are BOTH pregnant.
Thankfully he had never heard of them, so we were safe on that score.

Jane had made a lovely salad for tea and we sat in their garden to eat it.

I was glad of the salad because the wedding was nearer and what with working in the city centre and our blue-chip companies and high-end clients I had been having far too many work lunches and I did have a wedding dress to fit into.

Talking about that it was time to broach the subject of Jane and her bridesmaid dress. I thought it might be an idea If we scrap her original dress and go for a contrasting colour to the other bridesmaids and get her a nice maternity one. Not being funny but the weight she was putting on she would need a tent and we still had two months to go to the wedding.

She agreed, and we decided we would start looking that weekend.

Yet again I was alone all weekend as Carl was sorting out the office in Derby now he had all the builders sorted he needed an office down there and staff.

We enjoyed the rest of the evening with no wedding, baby or work talk, we just reminisced about the good old carefree days and how we couldn't believe we were all sensible and grown up. Well grown up!

It was getting late and yet again Carl had an early start, I wasn't bothered I was ready to go home and eager to spend a bit of quality time with my man.

It still gave me a thrill every time we turned the corner to our house, I loved the street and loved the house.

I went to get a quick shower before I got into bed and when I got to the bedroom, there was Carl, fast asleep!

All he seemed to do these days was work and sleep, we hardly saw each other, and I thought it was about time I had a word with Bob to see what he thought.

After work the following day I called in to see Bob, he was pleased to see me, as always and made me very welcome and I couldn't believe how much Scamp had grown, he was such an adorable dog and he had lost all that puppy giddiness and was just a loyal friend and companion now and followed Bob everywhere.

"I'm really worried about Carl Bob, all he seems to do is work and sleep, we don't seem to get any time together and I am not moaning I know the business is going really well, I am just worried he is doing too much" I said concerned

Bob explained that when you are starting or growing a business it is imperative to put all the hours god sends in, to do the ground work. Once it's up and running you can then ease the strain and that was where we currently were. Carl had been interviewing for staff in Leeds and Derby and getting the right people in place, showing them the systems and way, they did things and Bob was sure that by the wedding it would settle down and I would get Carl back.

I did feel awful talking to Bob about it, almost like I was moaning and not grateful at all for everything he had done for us, but I was just concerned, everything was going perfect and then it all just happened at once. We had the home and spare money, a wedding planned but I felt there was no point if I never saw Carl. I understood fully what Bob was saying and I really did appreciate everything he has done and is doing for us, so I decided to invite him for his tea tomorrow- 6.00pm sharp and told him he had to bring Scamp.

I left him looking happy with Scamp at his side.

On the drive home I got quite emotional that Bob had never been a Dad, it was very sad, and he would have been amazing at it. I had a Dad, but Bob was like my second Dad, he would never replace my Dad, but he was the closest thing to him.

As I sat at my desk the day after I had already decided what I was making Bob for his tea, it was warm, but he loved his bacon, so I thought I would do a salad with bacon and chicken. He would like it and I would make sure there was enough chicken left for Scamp.

The drive home was reasonable, I had left ten minutes earlier than usual and it hadn't half made a difference with the traffic and I was home in no time. I put the chicken on and put the bacon under the grill. Opened all the windows and put the radio on. I loved days like this, cooking and pottering about in my home. Ok so my kitchen was still tiny, but Carl and Bob promised it would be sorted after the wedding, I hoped so too as I didn't want all that building work going on when I was pregnant. You see, we had decided that we would try for a baby on our honeymoon. Why wait!!!

The thought thrilled me, and I was lost in those thoughts and totally lost track of time. My heart skipped a beat as I realised it was ten past six. That's not like Bob to be late, that was his pet hate to be late. I had better call him and make sure he hadn't fallen asleep.

I rang his number and was just about to start panicking when it was answered, oh thank god for that, for a second I had an awful thought.
"Hi Bob, its Jane, have you fallen asleep, you silly bugger or had you forgotten you were coming to mine for tea?" I laughed.

"No............can't.......... not right....... this, this" said Bob.

What was going on, he really didn't sound right, and I knew immediately something was wrong, oh shit what do I do, I needed to get there quick.

"Bob listen to me, I am on my way, don't worry I will be with you in a few minutes, now go find Scamp and go sit down and wait for me to come and I won't be long, I promise" I said, and I hung up the phone

What the shitting hell can I do??? Panic rising in me, I called my Dad and basically said Bob wasn't right and can he meet me there now.

I turned everything off in the kitchen, closed all the windows, grabbed my car keys and set off for Bob's. Luckily the traffic was mainly going in the opposite direction, so I got there in quite good time just as my Dad was pulling up.

I didn't think to talk to my Dad, I just needed to get to Bob to check he was ok. Luckily the door was open, and I knew exactly where he would be, in the sun room. I ran over and he just looked confused to see me and very tired.

"Bob are you ok my love, how are you feeling" I asked him "Ok just tired, very tired" slurred Bob

He sounded drunk, but I knew he wouldn't be. I looked around for my Dad, no sign, "Dad" I shouted I really was panicking now as I knew the signs, the confusion the tiredness, I think Bob was having a stroke.

"Now stay there my love I am going to see where my Dad is" I said to Bob letting go of his hand.

"DAD" I shouted again and ran into the hall.

He was on the phone to the ambulance, they were on their way. Apparently, Dad had thought the same as me and rung straight away.

"You stay with him and I will stay on the phone, keep him calm and comfortable" said Dad

I went straight back to Bob and just sat holding his hand and talking a load of shite. Dad appeared but still on the phone "Bob, can you put your hands above your head" asked Dad, he was being guided by the woman on the other end of the phone

Nothing, "Can you stick your tongue out mate?" asked Dad again while both me and Dad were doing the actions he was asking Bob to do.

Nothing still, Dad disappeared again, and I am guessing to replay the news to the ambulance woman on the phone.

He appeared again to let us know the ambulance was on its way and off he went the end of the drive to guide them in.

I was still sat with Bob and it was heart breaking, he looked very old suddenly and very scared. He just sat there staring at me, unable to speak and just looking confused. I carried on talking and tried to keep things very light.

The next thing I knew the ambulance men had arrived, they asked all the usual questions and then one of them steered me into the kitchen where my Dad was, I presume to work on Bob. They asked various questions like when anyone last saw him, what medication was he on, did he seem ok when we last saw him and off he went.

The ambulance man came back into us and asked me to contact anyone I thought should know as they confirmed what me and Dad had feared. They think he had had a stroke and were taking him straight into hospital and did one of us want to go with him.

Dad and I were in shock and just stared at each other.

They wheeled Bob out on a stretcher, he looked so frail and really upset. Scamp was following and whimpering. Oh god this was heart breaking.

Dad said "You go with him, I will take Scamp to ours and I will ring Carl and tell him what has happened. When you know anything ring me at home straight away and I will keep in touch with Carl". Thank god Carl had a work mobile phone which meant we could contact him when he was away from home.

I left with Bob and the ambulance crew and we were blue lighted straight to the hospital.

"Don't worry love, we will be there in a few minutes and they can take better care of him, because we can't say for sure when he started being ill, there is very little we can do but the hospital will do everything and don't be scared of the blue lights we use them just to get through traffic sometimes it's not always life and death" said the lovely ambulance man.

We got the hospital and he was rushed straight through and I was steered to a nurse who asked all the same questions as before. I was directed to a waiting room and told I would be kept up to date with what was happening.

I sat and sat for what seemed like an eternity and I prayed to God and Allah and anyone else I could think of just to help Bob and make him pull through.

I thought about Scamp and how upset he was, fretting that his master wasn't well. I thought about Carl who would be devastated and prayed he would drive safely and not panic.

Eventually a doctor came in and explained that he had had a massive bleed and that unfortunately they couldn't stop it in time.

They had done a full CT scan and it damaged a lot of his brain. He would be in hospital for quite a while but would be undergoing physiotherapy and speech therapy if necessary but for now they have given him a mild sedative to help him sleep and they would know more in the morning.

I couldn't even go see him as they moved him to a ward and they didn't want him waking, he needed to rest. I started walking out, in a world of my own, unsure what to tell anyone and just so shocked that someone's world could be turned upside down so quickly. Poor Bob.

I found a payphone and called my Dad. He said Carl was on his way and should be there any minute. I explained I was on my way out and asked if he could call Carl back and ask him to meet me at the entrance.

I got outside and reached straight into my bag for my comfort blanket, my fags, I didn't smoke much now as we were going to start to try for a baby after the wedding and thought it would all help, but I needed one now more than ever.

I think I had two on the trot and was just dying the second out when I spotted Carl, I ran straight over to him, threw my arms round him and broke down. We stood there, both of us sobbing and clinging onto each other for dear life.

Eventually I pulled away, I could see how upset Carl was and I just said, let's get to my Mums and get Scamp.

We pulled up at my Mums and she was straight out and threw her arms round us both, why she couldn't wait till be got inside I don't know.

We sat playing with the dog and explained everything the doctor had said to me. We will know more tomorrow when all the doctors have been, and more tests results are back. I said I would ring the hospital at ten o clock the following morning and hopefully we would know what to do from there.

We stayed for a while at Mums, but we were all still in a state of shock. He had seemed so well the day before, he wasn't a massive drinker, not overweight etc but that is what a stroke is, it's the unexpected to the unexpected and it has no age limit or time span it just comes for you and grabs you.

Dad had asked if he could keep the dog at theirs, as he seemed settled and Mum and Dad would be with him all the time as they didn't work. Plus, I think my Dad had grown quite fond of him already. He always did love dogs, but my Mum had always said no, I think though if any dog would make you soften, it would be Scamp.

Chapter 24

I got to work early the next morning to find DC already in.

I had explained what had happened and he said to take all the time I needed. It was mainly so I could make a few phone calls and maybe nip up to see Bob in my lunchbreak as the hospital was within walking distance of the office.

I knew there was no point ringing the hospital before 10 but I am sure time had stood still that morning, either that or the clock had stopped!!! Which it hadn't as I had checked about 14 clocks and they all said the same 9.47am

Go for a wee I thought, that will pass a bit of time and go for a smoke in the kitchen and make a coffee. Yes, that's what I will do, so I did and got back to my desk at 9.58. I sat and stared at the clock and as it turned 9.59 I just thought fuck it and I rang, ENGAGED!!!! I left if a while and tried again.

I eventually got through and spoke to someone at 10.17am, I was put through to the ward and spoke to a lovely nurse who said we might be best if we come in and see the doctor as he would be able to explain things in more detail. I arranged an appointment for that lunchtime.

I rang Carl and explained I would go and no need for him to go, his job was to keep Bob's business going and I would do the rest.

I got out of the appointment at about 3pm and rang DC to say I wouldn't be back at work but I would make the time up, he was fine and said to go home, digest it all and work on a strategy plan. I wasn't sure if he meant for work or Bob, as he loved talking in riddles, tit!

I drove straight to my Mum and Dads and thought by explaining it all to them first I could get it straight in my head before I had to tell Carl.

I pulled up and suddenly felt very nervous and I don't know why.

My Mum waited this time, until I got inside to throw her arms around me, maybe she didn't see me pull in.

She made us all a proper coffee, with steamed milk and everything and then came and sat down with me and Dad in the lounge.

I noticed straight away Scamp still looked lost, but my Dad was besotted and doing his best to cheer him up.

I explained exactly what the doctor had said. He had had a severe stroke and it had affected him quite badly, his speech had been affected and his walking and he had to learn everything again. Even just the basics like going to the loo, dressing and washing himself and making a cuppa.

It would mean a lot of very intense physiotherapy and speech therapy and he would be in hospital for quite a few weeks, but he had age on his side, he was early sixties, so not old at all and he had a determination, lots and lots of determination and he was still here. He would be telling the tale before we knew it. It did mean however he wouldn't be at our wedding which was a massive shame, but he would get better and we would have a party on his return home.

"So, we need to draw up a rota for visiting" said my Mum, "It's always left to the same few, so we will get that sorted and we will have the dog until Bob is home so that's not an issue and me and your Dad will keep an eye on the house and go every other day, or even every day, it's not far" said Mum, her mind working overtime with things to do.

In times of need my Mum was amazing, she was amazing anytime really, but you know what I mean. She was so practical it was amazing, I don't know what we would have done without her or my Dad. In fact, once we had let everyone know they were all amazing, all the lads at work went to see him, all his friends at the pub, my family all went so he was never short of a visitor.

The first time I went to see him after he had been taken in really shook me up, I know the doctor explained everything to me but when I got there he was like a cabbage. Not moving or talking, just laid there staring. I knew he was taking everything in, you could see it in his eyes.

I told him all about Scamp and how well he was being looked after, how his house was being looked after and his business and basically anything else I could think of to say.

It is very hard visiting someone who cannot talk, very one way and difficult to think of things to say. I would read the paper to him once I had filled him in on all the soap gossip and just general gossip.

Time to the wedding was getting nearer and nearer and at first, I didn't know whether to talk about it in front of him, but then I thought, well by not talking, won't stop it happening and it's something for him to look forward to seeing and hearing about and celebrating when he gets better.

I called in most days, as I worked so near, and my Mum bless her had everyone else organised to make sure Bob had a few visitors each day.

I kept in close contact with the doctors and nurses and they let me know his progress each day. He didn't smile now and that was devastating, he was always such a smiley person, but I had read on one of the leaflets in the hospital about strokes it is not just physically things change but people's personalities could also change.

It was just heart breaking to see this once such a happy carefree man was now laid in front of me with what looked like a tommee tippee cup, so he could have a drink.

One day I called in to find his bed empty, Jesus! I was just about to panic when a nurse came rushing in, I was just about to call you, we have managed to get Bob a bed at Jimmy's and they specialise in rehabilitation and physio, it only just came up, so we had to get him there quick sharp.

Phew I thought! Jimmy's wasn't too far, and I probably could still do it in my lunch hour but who knows not long to the wedding and honeymoon so by the time we are back he might be back home, you never know.

I got the details and decided to ring that night, the nurse explained the journey would tire him out and he would need his rest.

I left it till I got home later that night to ring the new ward and find out how he was doing. He was fine and settled and very tired. The nurse also explained that because he will be having a lot of physio the majority will be through the day, so any visitors might be best at night between 6 and 8.

Fair enough I thought.

Carl eventually walked through the door and again looked exhausted! I filled him in on Bob, he was pleased. Then he had his tea, had a bath and went to bed.

It's a good job I understand what is going on and understand why he is working all the time otherwise I would be well pissed off, well I was but I couldn't show it.

The wedding was a week away, I had decided on not having a hen do as Jane was preggers and I had a sneaky feeling my sister was, but she wasn't saying anything.

We had a meal at my Mums and a couple of bottles of wine and the boys went into town. It was just what Carl needed, a good night out with the lads and I think it was about 4am when there was a knock at my door to find my husband to be on the front step and his best man (Dave) laid on the drive and a taxi driver that wanted paying!!!

You should have seen me trying to get those two in the house without making a noise, I am very surprised I didn't pull anything, god they were a dead weight both of them and all either of them could do was laugh and say how much they loved me!

Don't you just love drunks!

I got them in, put them in the living room, threw two duvets at them and went back to bed. They were still there when I got up a few hours later. I don't think either of them had moved, I did go check and they were both still breathing.

Jane came around about 9 and they were still spark out, so we made a massive "kill or cure fry up" As soon as it was on the table we heard movement. They both appeared, looking like shit and very rough.

As they sat down and looked at their breakfast in front of them Jane and I stifled a giggle we were sure it would tip them over the edge but they both looked at each other, raised their cups of tea, said cheers and tucked into the fry up.

They had been playing us all along, they knew what we would do so they both had a nice long lie in and waited for us silly arses to make a full fry up, they were absolutely fine and pissing themselves laughing telling Jane how I struggled to get them inside last night and didn't I wonder how they had told the taxi driver where to take them if they were in such a state!!! For god's sake he was in on it too.

"It cost us an extra fiver for him to play along but it was worth it" howled Carl

"Great and I had to pay for the ride" I said.

We had well and truly been had but it was worth it just to see Carl laughing again.

We had a lazy day the rest of the day then at night both Carl and I went to see Bob and I have to say he looked a bit brighter and was trying to say a few words. The therapies were obviously working, and we think he said he wanted a coffee so I went down to the lobby to get us all a coffee.

As soon as I got back up I passed it to Bob and he took a drink, looked me straight in the eye and said, "Fuck me."

Carl looked at me and I looked back at him, what had he just said, I didn't know whether to laugh or cry. Bob never swore, I don't think I have ever heard him use that phrase, but he was talking I suppose.

"Bob, you can't say that, sssh" I whispered, and he looked totally confused.

He was definitely getting stronger each day, but the swearing was something else "

Chapter 25

The day of the wedding had finally arrived.

I'd been told I was stopping at my Mum's the night before and Carl had stopped at Jane and Dave's.

My Mum had loved having me back for one night, I could just tell, especially when I left a cup in the sink and didn't put it in the dishwasher, it was the little things that I am sure she missed.

We were up, breakfast all sorted and put away before the hairdresser or photographer arrived. Mum was very organised, and everything had to be just so.

I know it sounds daft, but it felt like something was missing with Bob still in hospital and still very ill it kind of took the fun out of it a bit.

That was until Dad popped open the champagne, we called Bob at the hospital, he was talking much better and after the phone call everything seemed to click into place and we were getting very excited.

Before we knew it, we were all just about ready to go.

The car arrived, I know this because my Dad was shouting and getting all giddy. He loved old cars, and this was AMAZING! An old black Mercedes Benz 300SC Roadster 1956 soft top and thank god for the weather, it was perfect.

I had always dreamed of a car like this for my wedding and didn't tell my Dad as I knew he would be too giddy.

My Mum went off with the bridesmaids and it just left me and my Dad. He filled up as I walked in the room and he told me how beautiful I looked, it would have been an amazing moment, but he spoilt it slightly by saying "Come on, chop chop, have you seen the car it's amazing"

We spent the whole journey with my Dad talking to the driver about the car!!! Not quite what I envisaged but it was very special.

We finally arrived at St Margaret's and the flowers looked amazing. As we pulled up I saw my Mum dart inside and take her place. The Bridesmaids were waiting and all that was left to do was go down the aisle and marry the man of my dreams.

As soon as I got out of the car my emotions overtook me and I welled up. I looked at my Dad and he just took my hand and said "Come on then, lets' get this show on the road"

All the way down the aisle I was trying to smile but tears just wouldn't stop – out of happiness but I was an emotional wreck. Luckily, I had a veil on and I don't think anyone saw.

The service was perfect, and Carl and I stood hand in hand and took our vows.

As we signed the register my Mum and Dad had arranged for a choir to sing, a gospel choir and what I could hear, they sounded amazing.

The bridesmaids all behaved and looked fantastic and before I knew it the Vicar announced, "I now pronounce you husband and wife" and the congregation let out cheers and were clapping! The whole thing was very upbeat and fantastic.

A few photos outside the church and then we had decided we would get some at the reception which was at the Low Hall, not far from the church and it was a large enough venue but small enough to feel very special.

As our call pulled up all the staff were there to greet us with a glass of champagne, for us, I don't mean that we all stood getting pissed.

The drinks reception was in full swing and Carl and I couldn't leave each other's side. We mingled with the guests and everyone said how beautiful I looked – ooh I could do with this confidence boost every day!

The toastmaster then announced that the guests were to take their places for the wedding breakfast. As they did so Carl and I were treated to another glass of fizz and we were both like big kids, so giddy and couldn't wait to get in but we had to wait for everyone to be seated. It was all done with impeccable taste and decorum.

At last we finally heard "Please be upstanding to greet your Bride and Groom" said the toastmaster and the guests erupted again with cheering and laughter and a slow clap that lasted until I sat down. I loved all this pomp!!!

The meal was ok to say we were catering for so many people but who cared as the drinks were flowing.

The speeches had us all crying and laughing. My Dad told stories of when I was a little girl and he used to walk up to pick me up from Brownies and if it was cold he would wear this green woollen hat (that my Grandma had knitted) and I would be so embarrassed by it and he promptly bent down and put the hat on – the actual hat!!! Hilarious and very touching.

Dave's speech was a quick run through of how we all met, things we had got up to from the start to the present day which had people rolling with laughter and then it was the turn of Carl. He did the usual thanking everyone and saying how beautiful everyone looked, thanked the bridesmaids and page boys etc and then he went on to say:

"Stood here now, looking round at you all I feel very honoured that you would all want to take the time out and celebrate the marriage of me and my beautiful wife, today, so far has been the best day of my life, not only have I gained another family I have also married my best friend and I am the happiest man alive."

He then continued to mention that we should also remember the people that couldn't make it today and he raised a toast to Absent Friends"

"All that is left to say is thank you from the bottom of my heart for sharing our special day and let's enjoy the rest of the day, lets P A R T Y !!!!" Carl shouted at the end

The cheers finally died down and the rest of the afternoon was spent outside in the gardens with everyone enjoying the sun and a few cheeky drinks, whilst the staff changed the room for the night reception.

Most people we invited came to the day do so there was only about another 25 to come to the night do, well we thought there was, but I think my parents and Carl's parents had got a bit giddy and ended up inviting quite a few other people, some of whom neither of us knew but who cares!

It gets to something when you are congratulated by people and as they move on you look at each other and say, "who was that"?

The evening reception was amazing, we did our first dance to Move Closer by Phyllis Nelson, it was "Our Song" and again it was just perfect. The night was amazing, but it went too quickly and before we knew it the big lights were on and it was time to think about going. Carl had arranged for us to go the Hilton for our wedding night, so we said goodbye to everyone and off we went.

As we got to the hotel there must have been a big do on as there were loads of people still milling around and they were all congratulating us and wanting us to join them, but we were both exhausted and couldn't wait to get to bed.

I couldn't understand at first how they knew we had just got married.

"Maybe it's the fact you have a wedding dress on, that might give it away" scoffed Carl.

As we got to the room I couldn't believe it, he had booked us a suite – it was bloody massive, with a separate sitting area, dressing room and a bottle of bubbly with the hotel's congratulations.

Well it would be rude not to enjoy it, so we did.

The bath was massive so what better way to enjoy our champagne than in the bath. We sat there for so long we had to keep topping the water up. We sat there talking about the day and how happy we were and how we couldn't wait to go on honeymoon – I had no idea where we were going but I couldn't wait anyway.

We were both missing Bob, but he was doing so well, and I think with a little bit of nursing and home care he should be home soon.

The morning after we had breakfast in our room and then got a call from the hotel reception to say our car was here for us when we were ready and not to rush???

Eh, had they got this right, we didn't have a car with us and we hadn't even thought about how we were going to get home.

We went down to the reception and they passed us a card that simply read:

I am not there in person, but I was with you in spirit and will be forever with you both every step of the way, enjoy the car, you have it for 2 days, don't go bloody stupid but enjoy it and don't be wasting it coming to see me

All my Love, Bob xx

Obviously, he hadn't written it, but he had obviously managed to communicate enough to get it all sorted, I was wondering if one of our family had arranged it with him. What a lovely touch so we were off and yes, the first place we went was to see Bob to fill him in on the day.

He did look so much better and I have no idea what they had been doing to him, but it was certainly working, he looked amazing.

I was talking to one of the nurses when she mentioned they would be moving Bob to a convalescent home to build his strength up and get him back into a routine and get him up and moving again and doing things for himself.

He really was so determined and even his talking was getting better, he would forget what he was meant to say but we all got the gist of it – it was a bit like a game of charades whenever he tried to tell you a tale.

We then did the rounds to the parents and we chatted about the wedding and how fantastic it was and then went home to pack to get ready for our honeymoon.

After leaving, we planned where we would go with the car the day after as we had one more day with it before we jetted off and I was still unsure where we were heading for on our honeymoon.

We decided we would take the car out for a spin to Haworth. We loved it there and there is a fantastic pub at the bottom of the main street.

I loved all the quirky little shops and obviously when you go there you must visit the Bronte House.

We got to the house and paid to go in and I don't know what it is but when I go somewhere like that, full of history and always very quiet I go into uber intelligent mode, well I try, and I look like I am reading and studying everything. So much so that as I walked up the stairs I noticed out of the corner of my eye a statue of a man sat on the window seat at the top of the stairs.

Must be the father or the son, I thought, so I went to look to see if there was any information on this person but as I did so the bloody statue moved!

Yes, your right, it wasn't a statue but just a visitor resting to get his breath.

I nearly shit myself and all hopes of looking intelligent soon disappeared as I let out a few obscenities.

The man in question was not amused and looked at me as if I had just shot his dog.

He tutted and walked away.

Hoping no one else saw it I thought I might manage to casually carry on and enjoy the rest of the house but no, I had been spotted and I knew this as Carl was doubled up, laughing his head off. So much so, he couldn't actually talk.

Time to go I thought.

And with that I gave Carl "The look" and went to bid a hasty retreat outside.

Still laughing Carl eventually caught me up.

"You never cease to amaze me, you make me laugh so much" laughed Carl.

We left and decided it was time to head home.

Chapter 26

I eventually found out where we would be honey mooning.

We were only going to the U S of A!! Yeah Baby and I couldn't wait.

We flew from Manchester to Los Angeles and had a few days looking around LA (that's what us locals call it) and The Wood (OK, so I made that one up) Hollywood.

Seeing the Hollywood sign was amazing and just as I had imagined it. I spotted it purely by accident, as were driving on the freeway. I nearly made Carl crash as I spotted it I shouted, "Hollywood Sign."

We went to the Chinese Theatre on Sunset and Vine and I have to say I was quite scared, it was a dump and full of weird people and as the sun set even more of them came out.

It's not every day you see Spiderman, on a skateboard, smoking god knows what and swearing at everyone as he skated passed them.

It was certainly an experience, but the best was the sightseeing tour – famous people's houses, it was good but to be honest most of the time all you could see was the fences around the huge properties. They are just normal streets though, ok so not as we know it but streets all the same and not as I had pictured them, to be in acres of land miles away from anyone, some were quite normal, though I guessed the prices wouldn't be.

We then did Rodeo Drive and that was AMAZING, the shops were to die for and we treated ourselves to a couple of very expensive watches and as we were buying they brought out champagne for us, that is when you know you are spending serious money.

It was an investment, as Carl said and a reminder of our honeymoon.

It was then time to move on to Vegas Baby!!!! Now that was an experience, the hotels got bigger and bigger as you went down the strip.

We were stopping in the Luxor which was near the start of the strip and it was a massive pyramid, very impressive but not so much when you got inside.

The lobby was ok but the rooms not so much. So much so, I had to complain, and we did get a free upgrade, then when I mentioned it was our honeymoon, they couldn't do enough for us. So, a word to the wise, a little complaint and a bit of information goes a long way.

We didn't really gamble but just walking through the casinos was amazing and so noisy.

One night we were sat in a bar in one of the casinos and got talking to the bar man who told us that they pump something in the air of the casinos to keep people awake, there are no clocks so you have no idea what time it is and don't feel you need to get home and a lot of the shopping malls and some of the hotels have painted ceilings of daytime and some of them just change.

The hotels were something else and each one seemed to get bigger and better as you went along and apparently if you come again there would be a new hotel – its changes that often and just gets bigger.

It was very humid as we were there but as we did some sightseeing, but it was nice to get into the air-conditioned hotels.

At night the choice of eateries was out of this world – you could literally choose whatever you wanted but once it got dark it got quite seedy and there were people handing out leaflets for prostitutes and you could get them to come to your hotel. You could see the helicopters flying them in and out!!!! It's a bloody different world!

I would say that I am glad we did it, but I was happy when we got back to California and this time to San Diego, outside LA was absolutely beautiful. The port was fantastic and had the most amazing yachts you had ever seen.

That was the most romantic part of the honeymoon, just very chilled on the beach and lovely meals at night and before you knew it, it was time for home.

It had been amazing, but I had missed everyone, and I couldn't wait to get back and try get Bob sorted.

We had found out the day before that he was doing amazing and he should be home within a week or two of our return, once all his care had been put in place.

He was walking now, but with a frame, he was talking but very slowly and had to really think about what he was saying. He was very weak, and I couldn't see that improving massively and he did get tired very easily and he was quite emotional at the slightest thing, even countdown would set off the tears.

Apart from that he was doing amazing to say that at first, he was a cabbage and couldn't do anything, he had done fantastic and we were all so proud of him.

My Dad was a regular visitor to him and now Bob was out of hospital my Dad would take Scamp up to see him and he cried did our Bob, bless him but to be fair stroke or not I think I would have if I hadn't seen my dog for that long.

My Dad had really got attached to Scamp and it wouldn't surprise me at all if him and Mum bought a dog once Scamp was back with his rightful owner.

So, we were ready for the off. We had had the best time, it was amazing to spend all that time with Carl as we hadn't been spending a lot of time together, what with Bob being in hospital and Carl's job.

We had really lived like kings and spent so much money, but we thought we would have this blow out as we were now officially trying for a baby, not that we told anyone, but we were.

It's not the kind of thing I could ever envisage telling people that we were actively trying for a baby, to me that was basically like saying "We are at it like rabbits" each to their own I suppose.

We had discussed it a while ago and I have to say I came off my pill just before the wedding, so it had time to get out of my system and all we had to do now was the extension to the kitchen and then I think we had done everything we wanted.

The journey home wasn't too bad and as soon as we walked through customs we couldn't believe our eyes; both our Mums had come to meet us!

Why do Mums do that – it is very sweet, but we just wanted to get home.

We had a coffee with them and then set off home, with them in the back of the car – I never thought to ask how they had got there!

As we were pulling on our street the Mums seemed to get more and more hyper.

It wasn't until we got down the drive I knew something had happened.

I ran around the back of the house to see why there was a skip on my drive and there she was!!! A beautiful kitchen extension. Bob had only pulled a lot of his staff off their jobs to get this knocked up for us and it didn't need planning permission due to the size.

It was fantastic and all freshly plastered and ready for the kitchen of our dreams – he had left us with a sink, cooker and fridge though and it looked strange in this huge room but that was our next task to pick a kitchen.

Well I thought it was but again Bob had got someone to come in and design a few for us and all we had to do was chose the cupboard fronts and which design we liked the best.

Now some people may see that as interfering but not us- we bloody loved it!!! saved us a job and it had obviously given Bob something to concentrate on.

The Mums were beside themselves with excitement and I don't think it really had anything to do with the fact we were home from honeymoon, but they were both pleased to see us.

The kitchen was easy to choose as Carl and I had a particular style in mind so that was all sorted.

My Mum told us my Dad was coming to pick the mothers up and she was making tea for 5pm and we were both invited.

It gave us time to unpack, take the extension in and just have that last bit of "Us time" before reality struck.

It was Soooooooooooo good to be home though.

Chapter 27

So, we eventually turn up to my Mums to meet up with everyone and discuss the wedding and our honeymoon.

When we pull up in the drive, I notice there are quite a few people there.

We walk in and are greeted by my sister and her brood, Jane and Dave, my Mum and Dad and Grandma.

The meal was lovely and we all seem to have discussed the wedding more than we needed when my sister announced that now that the wedding is all done and the honeymoon she has some news "We are pregnant"

For fucks sake there it is again "We" fucking we! No Lilly, you, are pregnant you just had help getting there!

Obviously, my Mum and Dad and Grandma already knew, this was just for our benefit.

Then Jane said, "Oh my god, congratulations, we are too!"

Stop it with the "we" already and Jesus Christ is this catching?

Obviously, we already knew, but none of the others did, so I suppose it was nice for her to tell, MY family, that SHE was pregnant.

So, it went from all about us to we are now, the only ones in the room that aren't pregnant and to be honest there was no sign of it either.

We were thrilled for both couples obviously but part of me was gutted and I was starting to get a bit worried. I know it hadn't been long but Christ, everyone seemed to be getting up the duff in no time at all.

The journey home was very quiet, and I am sure Carl was thinking the same as me. We just had to forget it now and it will happen when it happens.

Chapter 28

So, we had received great news, Bob was coming home.

He had got a lot stronger and was doing really well. His speech was still quite poor, but he was here and that is all that mattered.

I had booked the day off work, ready for Bob coming home. It had been a long process getting to this stage, carers would be coming in 4 times a day to help him but not to do things for him just to aid and prompt him.

Mum and I had been to Bobs the weekend before he came home to give the place a proper deep clean. We had got all his favourite food in and generally just made sure his home looked beautiful.

The hospital had provided quite a lot of equipment for him, grab handles, Zimmer frames, toilet risers – which were amazing, but my feet did dangle when I sat on the loo now, bed rails and a fall detector which basically was like a watch, but should Bob be in trouble he could press it and it would contact help or should he fall it would set it off and contact help. It was just peace of mind for us really that when he was on his own there was always backup.

He was here, the hospital was dropping him off and the carers would be round in the next hour to introduce themselves and speak to us all to see exactly what care he required.

Carl couldn't have the day off, he had been spending more and more time at work and now that they were branching out, it was more than ever but Mum and I were there, and Dad was calling in after he had pottered about at home.

Really, he wanted an hour or two on his own, away from anyone just to chill and get over him having to give Scamp up.

Bob looked quite well, but very tired. You forget that being indoors all this time takes its toll on you, once you come outside.

We got him sat in the sun room in a new high back chair (easier to get in and out of) got him a coffee and a biscuit and then went to get Scamp from one of the neighbours.

We decided it was best to let Bob get settled before we let Scamp see him, god forbid he would have knocked him over, that is the last thing we needed.

Now I am not a particularly soft gooey person but the sight of Scamp coming in the house and spotting his master was heart-warming. He kind of ran in, straight to the sun room, spotted Bob and went ballistic, it was so cute, and Bob was just crying, tears of joy!!! It was beautiful.

The carers came and explained that for 6 weeks they would be coming to assist Bob in everyday things like getting up and dressed, showered, shaved, meal making and general care of himself.

They seemed like lovely people and very caring, which I guess you would have to be if you were in the profession.

They were to come on a morning to get him up, lunchtime, dinner time and bedtime. They are hoping that over time this could be reduced as he gets stronger.

My Dad turned up with fish and chips for us all, from Slaters obviously, they were amazing, and Bob was thrilled.

The afternoons comings and goings had taken its toll on Bob, he was absolutely shattered and said he might have a little snooze in the sun room, so we left him to it. I said I would call back in an hour or two.

Mum said it's important to let him have time on his own, he had been with people full time for the last few months and it was his time now to kick back and reflect on it.

I got back home and pottered about for a bit, but I couldn't get Bob out of my mind. The fact that a few months ago he was fine and then within seconds how a stroke can change someone's life completely.

The brain is a fascinating thing, almost like a car engine, if one thing is blocked or damaged it effects the rest of the car, or body in this case. The specialist had explained that the brain is so clever that when it receives an injury it finds another path to start working again. Physiotherapy and speech therapy are so important to help the brain find a new path and I guess that's why sometimes it can't always do what it did before, or it can but slightly different.

I have heard of someone that had a particularly bad stroke and when they started to get better they could speak only in French and had to learn English all over again. Now I'm no doctor and not sure how true it is but it kind of makes sense.

It was time to head back to see Bob and see if the carers had turned up, I think the afternoon ones will have been and gone and we weren't sure what time the night time ones were coming, so I thought I would go check on him and wait to see the carers.

I got to Bob's and saw a car in the drive and guessing it was the carers I shouted "Hi Bob, only me" as I walked in.

I introduced myself to the man stood in front of me and he in turn introduced himself. He was Steve and he had been assigned to put Bob to bed every night during the week and they were just trying to work out the best time for both of them.

Steve obviously had to fit it into his working day and I don't think Bob was being particularly helpful. That was something else I had noticed, Bob had become quite short tempered and a little argumentative, but I guess it's only to be expected.

Bob was trying to say that 9.30pm was too early for him as he liked to watch TV. I guessed that as he was shaking his head, pointing at the clock and at the TV so I said it back to him.

"Do you think half nine is too early Bob?" I asked.

"Bloody yes" shouted Bob.

"Well the thing is Bob, Steve is here to help you and not upset you, he is trying to help, so why don't we move the TV from the kitchen into your bedroom, Steve can come and help you to bed and I am sure he will carry a drink into your room for you and you can get all comfy in bed and have a cuppa and watch TV, that way you are happy and Steve is happy that you are happy" I said in my best patient voice - you see, I can be caring, sometimes.

"Bloody shite yes" said Bob, now you would think that meant no and I would have too if I hadn't realised he was nodding his head and smiling.

"Well that's sorted then, I'll move the TV now and Steve can help you get ready for bed, I know its early now Bob but tomorrow (and with this I motioned with my arm to tomorrow, like you do) A bit like yesterday is pointing behind you!! (we are a very peculiar race sometimes!) it will be half nine, is that ok then?" I enquired."

I didn't get an answer, but I was guessing as Bob was trying to get up out of his chair that was him saying "that would be splendid my dear, let's get sorted then I want to get comfy!"

Now by the time Steve and I had moved the TV, got Bob ready for bed, put the TV in Bobs room, where he could see it, put a table at the side of his bed for his drink and a biscuit and the controls for the TV, we were knackered and I joked with Steve on the way out that he must be fit to do this day in day out and he just laughed and said how much he loved it and he felt honoured to be working with the majority of his patients and that knowing he was helping them to live a normal life at home was worth all the running about.

I really did admire people like Steve and I am sure they are not all nice sweet people like Bob, yet I just knew Steve would treat them all the same, with the dignity they all deserved. Round of applause for all our wonderful carers doing this job, they are amazing people. I had only had a brief insight into it for half a day and I was ready to drop already.

The drive home got me thinking again, when Carl and I had a baby, would we be able to spend as much time with Bob? Would we ever get pregnant, oh Jesus Christ now I am saying it – would we get pregnant, let me rephrase that, would I ever get pregnant!!! Phew that's better. With the amount Carl was working now and the amount of time I wasn't seeing him, it would be a miracle!

I got home, made a cup of tea and decided to run a bath. I liked nothing better than laying in my beautiful deep bath.

I had just got in when I heard Carl's van pull onto the drive. It must be past 10! This is getting silly now because I knew he would come in, probably take my bath water and go straight to bed. Well the miracle wasn't going to happen in this house anytime soon!

I was right, "now then gorgeous" said Carl, followed by a kiss on my head, "Save us your water, I'm shattered, ooh is this tea fresh" and as he said it he downed the whole contents of the cup and started getting undressed.

Now I know I said my bath was deep, but it certainly wasn't going to fit us both in and quite honestly looking at the colour of Carl, I wasn't sharing a bath with him the muck tub, the joys of being married to a hands-on builder. If he didn't come home covered in plaster dust or brick dust, then he had had a shit day.

"Good Day Love" I said, as I walked out of the bathroom not really caring for an answer, but I could hear him get in the bath, moan it was too hot and start chattering to me. I did the usual "Oh right" and "lovely" every now and again to make him think I was listening and then I heard "So I will be away for a few nights every week for the foreseeable, but you will be ok now Bob's home" said Carl and carried on but I didn't really listen to the rest I had heard all I wanted.

I wasn't married to fucking Bob, I didn't want to spend all my time with bastard Bob, I had my own fucking life and I wanted to spend it with the love of my life and not be a part time fucking wife. For fucks sake we were barely married, everyone I knew was pregnant and I wasn't, and it didn't look like I would be any time soon and I certainly wasn't going to get pregnant by that twat wallowing in the fucking bath anytime fucking soon now was I!

Did I say all this? Did I bollocks I simply said oh well you need to do what you need to you and I went downstairs to raid the fridge and get a glass of Baileys.

Fuck him, I didn't give a shit and then I went into the top cupboard in the corner of the dining room, got a chair and pulled it over to it, reached inside and pulled out a packet of Benson and Hedges and a lighter and I sat at the bottom of the garden with a Baileys and a fag and I thought Fuck you Carl, the fucking builder, and fuck having a baby.

I am sure it's over rated anyway, and you get fat and obviously drinking Baileys and stuffing a Cornish pasty down your gob doesn't, well not if you're having a fag at the same time! I sat there for ages, well three fags worth and only one top up of Baileys and I was feeling very sorry for myself.

I turned around and looked at my beautiful home, all lit up, I was young, and I had all this, and I was so lucky, and It was all because Carl, my wonderful husband worked so hard and provided this for me, for us, Yes, I had a good job, but to be fair my money kind of paid for nice things, fanny things that we didn't really need but were a must have.

I realised then that I was being silly, so I downed the rest of my drink, had the last drag of my fag and went back up to the house. I put my glass in the sink, looked at what was going to be my perfect kitchen, told myself to stop being so silly and to go upstairs and make it up with Carl.

I nearly ran upstairs and feeling all happy and warm inside (possibly the two large glasses of Baileys) I hesitated before I threw the bedroom door open, when I heard the familiar noise of my OH SO WONDERFUL FUCKING HUSBAND, SNORING!!!!

Well you can stick your happy ever after up your arse, I thought. I'm off in the spare room and I did, fuck him!!!!

I tossed and turned all night, not so much with guilt at what I was thinking but more the combination of a Cornish and two Baileys and a few fags when I hadn't smoked in such a long time, that niccy rush is a bugger never mind the food and drink. I would never do that, well not on a work night!

I got up early the next morning hoping I hadn't missed Carl and I went downstairs just as I saw his van pulling out of the drive. Well I hadn't completely missed him, but he certainly hadn't missed me, I don't think he even realised I hadn't slept in the same bed as him.

I spent most of the day at work trying to figure out what to do. Even if I did get chance to get pregnant, was now really the best time, with him working away so much. We had everything we ever wanted but it came at a price, we hardly saw each other and what was the point if we never saw each other.

It wasn't even as if I could tell Carl all this as I hardly saw him.

I couldn't tell my Mum because she would twitter and worry, I didn't want to admit to anyone at work, as I was perfect and had this perfect life, why spoil it for them.

I couldn't tell Lilly, she was too wrapped up in sprog number 2 to give a shit and Jane was like my arse at things like this and even more so since she found out she was pregnant.

She was pathetic, she could only manage a few hours at work as she was soooooooooooooooooo tired and I wouldn't understand how tiring it was being pregnant "The baby is literally taking ALL MY ENERGY YOU KNOW" she had said, about 674 times to me. "I am just soooooooooooooooo exhausted."

Get a grip girl because this ain't gonna get any better for the foreseeable, you first put on at least 4 stone, get varicose veins and piles, you won't be able to see your fanny never mind your feet, they will be swollen and sore, you then have to part with the baby, which I have heard is like passing a melon through your front bottom which I am sure must smart a bit , then your boobs fill with milk and burn and leak all over, then you have sleepless nights and they cry for no reason and shit everywhere, then they get their teeth and are mardy little shits, then they grow up, terrible two's and three's and they turn into a teenager, cost you a fortune and make your life a misery, so get a grip kid it sounds shit !

Basically, I wouldn't be telling her any time soon.

I couldn't speak to Bob either, he would only worry, I couldn't tell my Dad because he would tell my Mum.

I am screwed, so I Just have to suck it up and get on with it!

I FUCKING HATE MY LIFE!!!!

Chapter 29

I called in on Bob on the way home, he was looking fab, he seemed to like the attention from the carers, so I just had a quick cuppa and was ready to go when his phone rang.

"Hello, hi love it's me, I thought you might be there, I was just ringing to see what time you were coming home" said Carl, on the other end of the phone.

Oh, you were, were you, well yes, I am here and then I am going to go the Fleece and having a couple of drinks with the locals from the garage. I'll leave my car there because I intend to get as pissed as a fart and then I will call and get a Chinese, eat it when I get in, which I have no idea what time that is so you might as well fend for yourself and go to bed and make sure you are asleep when I get in because it would be very awkward to have a conversation with you as I barely fucking know you now, so trot off to bed and FUCK OFF. I only thought that and then I said "Oh I'm just leaving now, are you at home? I'll see you in ten minutes" I sang and put the phone down.

What a whimp!

I said bye to Bob and set off home.

Paranoia set in then on the drive home, why was he home?

Why did he wonder where I was? What was he up to? Oh god I bet he's leaving.

Before I knew it, I had pulled up on the drive, I felt sick to my stomach.

I sat in the car for what felt like seven hours, it was only a few minutes, but I am building the tension here!

I finally got out and walked down the drive. As I went to put my key in the door it opened and there was Carl, all clean and smelling divine, he had a very dodgy pinny on – one that the mother had obviously bought us from some church fayre – and the biggest smile on his face.

He bent down to kiss me and grabbed my hand, pulled me towards the dining room. There was the table all set, and I could smell something delish coming from the kitchen.

"I am sorry sweetheart for last night and for the past few months, I have been a right tit and not made any us- time but I am going to change that, starting from now. I'll still be away for a few nights a week, but I promise the nights I am at home I will be at home at a normal time and we will have our time together, I have missed you so much and love every ounce of you.

Now come and sit down, I've cooked, and I've got some of your favourite wine and I bought some of that vanilla ice cream you like for pudding, I was going to put some Baileys on top, but we seem to have run out!

He had me with the smile at the door, but the mention of Baileys turned my stomach for a second.

I LOVE MY FUCKING LIFE and I love Carl. It's like he read my mind, or read my thoughts, he is a little sweetie and the night was perfect, it you get my drift.

Now picture crashing waves and thunder and lightning and skip nine months forward.

Now that IS too obvious!

Let's try a couple of months down the line, we were still having a lot of US-TIME, it was perfect, Carl was coming home on time, he was still working away but it's amazing how soon you get into a routine.

The guy at Block Busters had now got that used to seeing me and knowing what films I liked, he used to get them ready for me.

He was either very good at his job or I had bored him stiff because I was quite bored from time to time but the "Pretty Woman" and "Breakfast Clubs" of this world had to be watched again and again and that's just what I did with my ME TIME!

I kept vising Bob, but I think even he was sick of the sight of me every night Carl was away as I upset his routine.

I could only stand going to the parents once a week, my sister and Jane were only on desperate times, my sister not because she was a pathetic pregnant person but she was a smug, happy, pregnant person with a full time husband and Jane, well she was just a bit slack and usually in bed when I called round at 7 and I didn't really have that much to say to Dave when she wasn't there He was a pathetic "my wife is pregnant husband." Like no one ever has had a fucking baby.

So, the three nights Carl was away I would do the parents one night, my Grandmas one night and we would do "Take a Break" puzzles and send them off and she would feed me the most amazing food ever, that had been slow cooked all day and ready as soon as I walked in, then I might have a chinky and a video night and a night at Bob's with Steve having a coffee with them both.

Then before I knew it my Knight in Shining Armour would be back with a bottle of the old vino and some choccies and usually an early night was on the cards if you get my drift, cue to crashing waves again!

It was all going so well when we got the all-important call.

"Your sister is in labour and in the hospital, you had better get over here now, your Mum needs you" said my Dad, when he called one night just as Carl had walked in on his first night home!

It wasn't that anything was wrong, it's just my Mum loved an audience when any drama was happening So with a quick kiss and a dash to grab the car keys, we both left to watch my Mum walk up and down the carpet in the living room for what could be hours.

"What took you so long, I'm sat here worrying about your sister, looking after your niece and your father is bloody useless" spat my Mum, as soon as we walked in through the door, not 10 minutes after my Dad called.

Poor Mum, having all that to do. Yes right, she was on the wine and my Dad was in the garden entertaining Louisa, you just sit there and feel sorry for yourself and get pissed mother, I thought!

Carl took his lead and went to join the garden gang.

Well if you can't beat them and so I helped myself to a glass of vino, cheers mother this is going to be a long night.

To be fair it wasn't that bad, Louisa was an absolute doll and had no idea what was going on but loved all the attention she was receiving. We jumped every time the phone rang, and it was about 8.30 that we received the call that baby James Junior was born weighing 8lb 7oz, mother and baby doing fine.

Louisa was in bed and we didn't think there was any point waking her up.

Dad opened the champagne to celebrate, we drank that and went home. It's a good job it was quick as I was feeling quite pissed after the red wine and the champagne.

It was me who fell into bed that night and fell straight asleep, not quite what I had in mind when I was planning Carl's return.

I rang work the next morning to take a bit of flexi, so I could nip in to see Lilly and James. I obviously called into the shop for the obligatory balloon and choccies.

Oh my god he was absolutely perfect, he looked like a little Winston Churchill minus the cigar and obvs a lot cuter.

Lilly was in for the next three days, so it was up to Mum and Dad to look after Louisa. I think they secretly loved it and it was amazing to see her playing in the forever house, my house, the house that hopefully one day my children would play in.

I rang Jane to tell her and all I got was how she wishes it was her, she still had so much time left until her baby was due and she was still so tired and so fed up and so fucking boring!

I swear to god I will not be like that when I am pregnant.

Talking about that, I think I had better call into the old chemist and get a test. I think I was due to come on last week. Since I stopped taking the pill I was all over the place, period wise and quite honestly had no idea so I think it was best if I did the test.

By the time I got home with test in my bag I was shaking, for Christs sake, man up woman! I read the instructions thirteen times and did as instructed and weed on the stick. I replaced the cap and timed the two minutes to the results.

I know everyone says it, but it really was the longest two minutes of my life. I decided not to tell Carl and that I wanted it to be a surprise and was planning how I would tell him. Wrap the test in a box for him to open and see the result? No that wouldn't work he wouldn't understand it. Bake a cake and put "We are pregnant on it?" I don't fucking think so! Oh god I had no idea.

Time up, one line to say the test had been completed and nothing else, not a hint of another line! Not pregnant! Oh well there's always another time.

Yes, right, I was trying to convince myself that I wasn't bothered but I was, and I didn't want to worry Carl and was it really anything to worry about just yet? It had only been 6 or 7 months! Some people took years, so I will try and put it to the back of my mind and carry on regardless.

So, I said I would take Louisa in to meet her new baby brother. She was so excited and just kept saying "Baby, Baby" She is adorable, and Lilly looked remarkably well for a woman that had her fanny cut from belly button to arsehole.

We called for a happy meal on the way home and Carl met us there, from the outside it would have looked like the perfect family, but obviously it's our niece not daughter.

Mum and Dad were ready for Louisa when we got back to theirs and I got a bollocking for letting her have a happy meal – "Its full of rubbish, it that muck" said my Mum.

Oh well if you can't spoil your niece when she becomes a big sister for the first time when can you.

We dropped her off, said our goodbyes and called to see Bob.

He looked dreadful and I am not sure if he had a water infection, he was very confused, and I was hoping it was a water infection and not another stroke. We decided to wait until the carers came to see what they thought.

Carl and I were worried, we felt awful for not having seen him in the last couple of days but what with Lilly having her baby and all of us trying to look after Louisa there hadn't really been time, plus Carl and I had started spending as much time together as we could whilst he was at home.

Steve turned up and we raised our concerns, he said not to worry and that he would put a note into the folder (where it was documented all about Bob, what he had eaten, his toilet and bowel habits and any concerns the carers had) for the carer in the morning and if they were concerned they would call his doctor.

We left feeling easier than when we first arrived.

It had come to that last night feeling again, only for 4 days but it was a horrible feeling. We made the most of it and would start the count down again.

The mornings of the last days were always hard to say goodbye but like Carl said four more days and we will be sat with a takeaway and a bottle of vino.

I went off to work, missing Carl already and planning my night. As I got to work I called the carers to see how Bob was. No one had been, so the lady on the other end of the phone said she would get Marie to call me when she was there. I was sat at my desk my phone rang and it was Marie.

"Hi Clare, It Marie, One of Bob's carers, I have a message to call you" said Marie.

She went on to say "Bob is ok but still a little confused, so we are going to call the doctor and that she would make sure someone was with him when the doctor came so they could explain what the issue was without Bob getting all flustered.

The rest of the morning went by without a hitch and then later that afternoon the Doctor rang. He said Bob was confused! 7 years in medical school Doc to tell me that!

We needed to make sure he drinks more, he had prescribed some anti biotics and that this kind of thing was to be expected with the brain injury Bob had received.

So, I came off the phone not really clear about what had happened or how he was, so I left work early thanks to flexi time, though I am sure I was in minus figures now and drove straight to Bob's.

He was very weak and still confused but the carer that was there had said he didn't want anything to eat which wasn't like Bob but then if you feel a bit shit, I have heard some people go off their food – for me that has never happened, and I am sure I would eat when I was asleep if I could.

I called to Morrisons on town street and got a few piccy bits and decided to have a little bit of food and maybe a glass of wine and then get a bath and go to bed.

As I pulled up in the drive Mr Archer was outside, he was a lovely man and he passed me some pears from his tree. We chatted for a while and then I went to make my tea.

As I laid in the bath that night I found myself puffing my stomach out to see what I would look like pregnant. I could cope with that, what's all the fuss about.

Tiredness came over me as soon as I got out of the bath, that or the heat of my bath and I thought I would just lay on the bed, in my towel until I came around.

I must have fallen asleep because I woke up frozen, I climbed into bed and fell into a lovely deep sleep.

I woke with a start, as I thought I could hear someone at the door, it was dark outside, so it must be late, I turned the light on and squinted at the clock – 2.45am and there it went again, a knock at the door.

I didn't really understand what was going on but just ran downstairs and I wasn't expecting what I found when I opened the door.

Chapter 30

Two policemen greeted me when I opened the door and asked if Carl was in, I explained who I was, and they asked if anyone was with me.

I explained the situation and they recommended I get someone round. I couldn't, my best mate was heavily pregnant, my Mum and Dad were knackered having had my niece for a few days and my sister had just had a baby.

"I am fine honestly, I can call someone later, but can you just tell me what has happened and why are you here" I said getting quite scared.

I knew it couldn't be Carl as they had first asked for him, oh god was it my Mum or Dad?

"Is there somewhere we can go to sit down Clare, I am afraid I have some bad news for you" said Policeman number 1.

"Erm, yes, yes, through here" I stuttered and threw myself on the nearest chair. I really was panicking now, this was not going to be a lottery win, that was for sure.

"We were called out to a property this evening and we are really sorry to have to tell you…….." and I don't remember what else they said after that, but I do remember them saying to me, "You are noted as Next of Kin and therefore I am afraid I will have to ask if you would be prepared to come and identify the body." said policeman 2.

I went into auto mode and started grabbing my keys until I realised they would be taking me, I went to get dressed and I joined the policemen back downstairs.

I don't think it had really hit me, I was actually laughing at the fact I was going to be riding in a police car and that I had never been in one and they were quite boring inside.

We chatted until we got to the property.

I think you are kind of in no man's land and not sure how to react.

We got the property and there was another policeman and Steve, the carer. Steve came straight over and hugged me, he was desperately upset.

It was Steve who had found Bob dead. He had been to see him earlier and said he wasn't right, but that Bob had insisted he left. Steve had gone home, and he said he didn't know why but he said, "I just had a feeling something wasn't right and when I pulled up outside, the ambulance and the police were already there."

Bob had felt unwell and pressed his fall detector which alerted a local call centre who dispatched an ambulance and the police. The ambulance was too late and unfortunately Bob was pronounced dead.

Steve said they tried everything but couldn't save him.

Poor Steve he really did seem upset. I busied myself by making us all a cup of tea and then I had to go identify Bob. He just looked like he was asleep. I confirmed it was Bob and asked what happened next.

Two of the original police said how sorry there were for my loss and excused themselves leaving me, Steve and the other policeman.

He arranged for a local undertaker to come and take care of Bob and that it was just a waiting game now. Steve said he would stay with me and help in any way and we told the policeman he could go. He said he would stay but he would stay in his car to give us some privacy.

Steve and I made another drink and just sat chatting about Bob, and he explained that he had taken to Bob the first time he met him, he said he reminded him of his own Dad and how he wished he had of known him before Bob had become ill. I told him just what he was like, very very generous and a true gentleman, he really will be missed by us all.

It was now nearly sunrise and I suddenly realised I hadn't let Carl know. Well there wasn't any point just yet, I would wait until the funeral director had taken care of Bob's body, I would sort Steve out and then go home and start letting everyone know.

Why didn't Carl and I go see him more? Why didn't we talk more, all these questions that I am sure everyone going through a loss says.

It also reminds you of other people that had passed, and I was very lucky that I had only lost my Grandad. Not lucky he had died but lucky that there had only been one.

Steve told me more about himself and how he got into care work, he was at Nursing college and did this to pay his way through. He lived alone and had moved up from Kent as

LGI was the largest teaching hospital and obviously the rent was so much cheaper. He really was a lovely bloke, he had a few friends up here but had only been up here 8 months so I said he was welcome at our house anytime and that we should all go out.

Steve used to be a solicitor but didn't really like the ethics behind it – sticking up for the bad guys as he put it and then his mother became ill, so he took that as a sign and left and looked after his Mum until she passed away, which is when he decided to get into nursing.

It was all so surreal, here we were drinking tea and talking about our past when the door went, and it was two funeral directors and the policeman again. They offered their condolences to me and Steve (which actually made us laugh as it was obvious they thought we were a couple) strange how you laugh at such silly things in times like this.

Before we knew it, poor old Bob was being carried out. We didn't see, they were very discreet and after they had gone we went to where Bob had been and that's when it hit us both, poor Scamp was laid where Bob had been, just crying, making such a sad sound, we both bent down to comfort the dog and broke down. Both of us and Scamp, all sat there crying.

"What are we going to do with Scamp" I asked Steve.

"Well I would take him and look after him for you, but I can't have pets in my flat" said Steve.

"Don't worry I know, my Dad will take him for now, until we decide what is best for him" I said hoping that my Dad would.

"I'll take him for now and worry about that later" I said.

Steve drove me home and we said our goodbyes and he gave me his home phone number, so we could keep in touch, I said to take mine from his work phone.

As I got home, Mr Archer from next door came out as Scamp and I got out of the car.

"Is everything alright my love, come in and have a cup of tea, I've just made a fresh pot" he said. He had heard the knocking and noticed the police car this morning and had worried something was wrong.

"I hope you don't think I am being nosey" he enquired.

I didn't at all, I knew he was being kind and I filled him in on all the details. He too offered his condolences and asked if there was anything he could do.

There wasn't anything anyone could do really until I had started letting people know.

Shit I really had better let Carl know now, he would be up already.

I went next door to my house, Scamp in tow and dialled Carls number.

"Bloody hells what's wrong with you have you set the smoke alarm off or shit the bed" were Carl's opening words.

"Carl love I am so sorry but there is no easy way to say this, but I think you might want to sit down" and I hesitated and then carried on and said, "Bob has died love, last night, very peacefully, are you ok?"

Nothing, not a sound, nothing. "Carl, love, are you there, are you ok?" I asked.

It was ages before he replied, obviously trying to stop himself getting upset he simply said, "I'm on my way home" and with that he hung up.

I rang Mum and Dad next and they too said they would come straight round, first thing my Dad asked when he walked through the door was "Are you ok love and where's the dog" This was the perfect chance to ask if he fancied a long-term lodger!

Of course, my Dad was upset at the passing of Bob but secretly delighted that he and his pal Scamp were to be reunited and I swear if dogs could smile Scamp had the biggest smile on his face. That was one thing sorted.

Mum was very organised in situations like this and took total control in ringing round and informing the few people we felt needed to know.

"We will stay with you till Carl gets back and then we will get off love and get Scamp settled" said my Dad.

Bless them, you can't beat your parents in times of need.

Carl was home just after 10, he must have literally put the phone down to me and set straight off.

My Mum and Dad said how sorry they were and what a lovely man he was and if there is anything they can do just to let them know and that they would leave us now, but they were in all day if we needed them.

No sooner had they pulled away did Carl break down and he cried and cried and cried, and I sat and held him as tight as I could. He saw Bob as a father, not that he didn't love his own Dad, or the man he called Dad, but he had grown up into the fine man that stood before me, with Bob by his side.

Bob had done so much for us, given us so many opportunities and he was part of our family and it was a massive loss to us all, this was going to be a very hard few weeks /months to say the least.

That day was a very strange day, there was nothing we could do really until we had the note to register the death.

Although physically Carl couldn't do anything to make anything better he thought it was only right that he told all the staff. Everyone thought the world of Bob, so he arranged for the local foremen to come to ours that night and he would tell them and then they could inform the rest of the staff, Jesus we couldn't have all the staff here there were loads of them now, up and down the country.

Carl thought it was best to have them come to ours, a bit more personal than sat in the pub or in the office and some of the guys that were coming had started out with Bob, they had only ever worked for his company or with him.

There were five of them that came, each of them had a special connection to Bob in their own way. Obviously like any profession when anything happens out of the ordinary they are all on the phone discussing what it could be, and this was certainly the case with these five as they all turned up together.

Mike, I think he is called said as he walked into the hall "So come on then Boss what's all this about, do we have a job or not?"

Speak your mind Mike, don't beat around the bush I thought.

"Come on through lads and don't worry, you have a job" said Carl trying to put them at ease.

"Can I get any of you a drink? Tea, Coffee? Beer?" I said also trying to keep things light.

"Well, none of us are driving so a beer would be grand" said spokesman Mike, I was beginning to wonder if the others could speak, but I got them all a beer none the less and one for Carl. I think they might be having a few tonight.

I sat at the side of Carl and put my hand on his knees as he started to tell them.

"Right lads there is no easy way in saying this" he hesitated and took a deep breath. "As you know Old Bob hasn't been too good, well I am just going to come out and say, I'm sorry lads but he passed away last night, it was very sudden, and they don't think he suffered at all. It looks like he had a massive stroke and it finished him off"

I have never seen so many men look as lost in my life.

They were all completely stunned. It was quiet for ages and no one really knew what to say.

I took the hint and went and got a few more beers and handed them out.

"I don't know what to say, I don't think any of us do, do we lads" said Mike and the rest of the lads shook their heads.

"Well there is one thing for sure, Bob would not want you all moping around and feeling sorry for him, he loved every second of his life and he is at peace with his beloved wife, June. It is a massive shock, but I propose a toast to Bob" I said as I raised my cup of coffee followed by chinking of bottles from all the blokes.

The conversations then started about things Bob had got up to over the years, the best one being a pub crawl they all used to do.

A Pub Crawl, they all put about £10 in a pot when they started and last man standing took the lot. Every year Bob walked away with the prize, none of the lads could understand it until one year he was rumbled. Bob was the first at the pub and he would order a half but in a pint glass and wait for the others to arrive.

He would drink up and say, I'll meet you at the next, I'll get the drinks in and he did the same in each pub, they would all get pints and he would get half but in a pint glass.

Each time they came in he was drinking off and onto the next pub. Feeling under pressure they would drink quicker than normal and meet him in the next pub and so it went on and on until Bob had had 10 halves to their 10 pints.

Clever eh! and yes, he did walk away with the pot but always put it in the charity box at the end of the bar in the last pub without anyone seeing.

The tales went on and on and I excused myself as the phone started ringing.

It was Steve to check to see if Carl and I were ok. I explained what was going on and told him to get himself over to join us, but he declined saying he was going for a walk up to the park.

I hung up after the conversation had ended and thought what a good idea and nipped into the dining room, told Carl what I was doing and going for a walk and put more beers out in front of them all.

As I walked up to the park I suddenly realised just how beautiful Horsforth was.

My street was lined with blossom trees and they looked fantastic, you could hear the distant hum of someone's lawn mower and the birds tweeting. It was a beautiful evening.

I turned the corner at the top of Victoria Drive and headed up to Horsforth Hall Park.

The Park had fantastic memories for me, as a child we would go watch my Dad play cricket there, hours were spent watching him. Well, we wouldn't sit and watch him, there was too much fun to be had with the other cricketer's kids, but we were there. My Mum was on the wives' rota to do the teas and coffees and sort the food out and the sweets, always a fantastic supply of sweets.

The Park also had an annual Gala and my junior school Newlaithes, would enter a float for the parade and I was on it each year. I was a Cat, a sea horse, Cinderella and Edward from Edward and Mrs Simpson. A different theme each year and I think my Mum dreaded me coming home each year once the theme had been decided as she had to sort a costume to suit.

As I got older and started at Benton Park, the park opened up a whole new world and a new group of friends. We would congregate there and either watch the lads breakdancing in the Band Stand, or we would play Wham on our ghetto blasters, each taking it in turn to bring theirs as the batteries for those things were very expensive.

Freedom by Wham was one of our favourites and even to this day when I hear it, it takes me back to the carefree days.

Before I knew it, I had reached the gates, I walked through and as I did I noticed someone sat on a bench hunched over, it was Steve. I approached and made myself heard as I got nearer. "I knew you would come up," he smiled.

I sat at the side of him and we both just sat and looked out over the park to the cricket pitch and the bandstand.

"There used to be a large manor house over there" I said pointing in the distance to the opposite side of the park from the cricket pitch.

"Really, what was it like" asked Steve.

"I'm not that bloody old, you cheeky git, it was years before I was born but I have seen photos of it and I think a relative of my Grandmas worked there, that's why it's called Horsforth Hall Park, it was the grounds of Horsforth Hall" I said feeling very knowledgeable.

"I still can't get my head around last night, it's all so surreal" said Steve.

He had taken this worse than I thought but then like I always say there is no right and wrong way to grieve, we are all different. Carl and the lads were getting pissed at home and Steve and I were sat in a park.

"I know what, let's go for a drink, the Fleece will be dead tonight so how about a quickie at the friendly – (the local name for the Horsforth Hotel).

We walked down to the pub and as it was still so nice I told Steve to get a seat and I would get the drinks and I had already decided I would get a packet of fags as well.

As I came back Steve looked a bit brighter. I sat down and went to light a fag. "Oh god, you have read my mind, I could murder one, do you mind if I have one" said Steve.

"Help yourself" I said, and we sat drinking and smoking, two of my favourite pastimes.

"I really appreciate you coming tonight you know" said Steve.

"I know you do but to be honest there is only you that I wanted to see tonight. I think it is because we were both there last night and you kind of have to relive it don't you" I said.

I explained again that Carl was grieving in his way with his work mates and we were doing this. We had a few more drinks and then we decided to call at the Regent for a bag of chips and scraps. You can't beat chips and scraps with loads of salt and vinegar out of newspaper can you.

As we walked, we got to the top of Victoria Gardens and sat on the wall to the car park and chatted about Bob and what there was to do.

It was getting late by now, so I gave Steve a hug, told him I would be in touch and I carried on down the hill and onto the other Victoria walk that led to my street.

As I walked on the street I wasn't sure if the lads would still be there, but it was obvious they had gone as there was no noise as I entered the house.

Carl was sat alone in the semi darkness in the dining room, with a beer in hand and just staring into space.

He jumped as I walked in, I don't think he realised I was there, he was that deep in concentration.

"What are your plans for tomorrow then, are you going back down south or staying up here "I asked him.

"I'll stay here for the rest of the week, until we get everything sorted. I will nip into the yard tomorrow and just check on the lads" said Carl.

With that he finished his beer, went to get another and sat back down, I yawned. "get yourself to bed, you've not slept, I'll be fine, and I'll be up in a minute" said Carl.

I didn't need telling twice, I kissed him on his forehead, told him we would get through this and went to bed.

I must have needed the sleep because before I knew it, it was morning and I hadn't even heard Carl come to bed.

As I went downstairs I realised why that would be, he didn't make it be bed, he was sleep in the chair. I shook him lightly and told him to go up to bed for an hour or two and that I would wake him up in a bit.

The last thing I needed is for him to be exhausted, he was a right mardy arse when he was tired.

I pottered about in the kitchen, like you do and thought about Bob, I made a coffee and thought about Bob, I sat and drank my coffee and thought about Bob.

I rang Steve to check he was ok, he was, we talked about Bob.

I rang my Mum and we talked about Bob.

Then the phone rang again, and it was the coroner's office, they were issuing the piece of paper, so we could register the death, it was official he had had a massive stroke.

I made a few more phone calls and we had an appointment to register his death the day after. That was that and as soon as I had that, I knew I could start with the arrangements for the funeral.

We had briefly discussed what we were thinking would be acceptable and what we thought Bob would want.

Luckily, I had my Mum with me and I knew she would help.

Chapter 31

The arrangements had been made and the day of the funeral had arrived. We were going from Bob's and the funeral procession was going to take Bob on his final journey from his dream marital home, past his empire and up to St Margaret's.

That church had seen us in there more over this last few years than ever before with births, deaths and marriages!

We had put an announcement in the paper as we were unsure if everyone knew.

I had gone through Bob's phone book and rung everyone I thought needed ringing, but he had put everyone's nicknames in his book, and I wasn't sure if Big Al, or O.B. or even Twinks needed to know but I let them all know anyway.

There was quite a few of us at the house, waiting for the hearse to pull up.

As it arrived, the funeral director requested that we all take our places in the various cars as we were to be setting off very soon.

It's so strange, I know I haven't been to many funerals, but walking passed the coffin just seems so unreal, is that person inside??

The first one I saw was my Grandads and I remember it did freak me out somewhat, whereas now, whether it's because I am older, it doesn't freak me out, but it is still quite strange, knowing that person is in there.

The journey to St Margaret's was just as we had planned, and we know Bob would love it, passed all his old haunts and his empire, his place of work then straight up to the church.

As we pulled up I was surprised to see so many people, but then Bob had lived in Horsforth most of his life and he knew everybody and by the look of it they had all turned up today as a mark of respect and to say their goodbyes.

The service was lovely, it was a humanist service as Bob wasn't a big believer in God. Carl said a few words about Bob, the fun times they had shared, a few funny stories and then he closed by simply saying, "You were like my second Dad, I loved you yesterday and I love you today and I always will, rest in peace my best Pal Bob.

It was beautiful and there wasn't a dry eye in the house, I was very proud of him for being able to do it, I don't think I could, not in front of all those people.

We had the funeral tea back at the house, we didn't want it to be a big boozy do and we thought it was nice for all his friends to say their goodbyes at his house, his beautiful home for so many years.

We had no idea what was happening with Bob's estate, but we said to his close friends, if there is any little memento they would like of Bob's, to take it. I am sure no one would mind.

So that was that really, not much else to say, it was a beautiful service and Bob would be proud. Steve helped Mum and I clean up after everyone had gone.

He had been amazing, and we had promised we would keep in touch and I think we will. He is so kind and caring and he thought the world of Bob in the brief time he knew him.

You couldn't not like Bob, he was a true gent.

Chapter 32

Back to normality then, both Carl and I back to work and I was super busy. We had taken on a few more staff as we were doing so well, which was ok but its more people responsibility for me, making sure they were all ok and doing an excellent job and that they all had enough work.

Appraisals were coming up, so I was keeping a close eye on them all, there were a couple of people that needed a kick up the backside, so I would be watching closely, like the true bitch I am.

Carl was as busy as ever now, doing 4 days away and 3 at home but it sometimes turned into 5 away and 2 at home, which I wasn't keen on, but it was what it was, so I had to get on with it.

As I got home that night there was an official looking letter addressed to both Carl and me. Carl wasn't home for a few days, so I wasn't going to wait until then, I made myself a coffee sat in the kitchen to open it.

As I sat and read it, I couldn't believe what I was seeing.

Not only had Bob signed over the rest of his business to Carl, he had also left us every bit of his estate. His house, his car, all his possessions, all his savings, you name it and we had been left it.

I didn't know what to do and I couldn't read the last bit for the tears in my eyes, he really had thought the world of us, as we did him, but that didn't stop me feeling heartbroken that he didn't have any family of his own to leave all this to but as Bob used to say, "You lot are all the family I need".

I rang my Mum straight away, she was in the bath! I didn't want to tell them on the phone I had decided, so I said to get the kettle on I was on my way over.

As I read the letter out to them my Mum had her hands to her mouth and my Dad just sat there and mulled it over in his mind.

"So, what do I do" I said confused.

"Well that is entirely up to you and Carl, but I would say you are both extremely wealthy people and you need to invest this wisely, we are talking life changing amounts here love, not just a few bob, excuse the pun" said Dad and I gave him the "not the right time look."

"I haven't even told Carl yet but is it something to tell him over the phone? He's not back for a bit, oh god I don't know what to do" I said and as I did so Dad passed me the phone and told me call Carl straight away.

I walked into the kitchen and as he answered I just broke down, I don't know why, shock probably at what I had just read.

I managed to compose myself "Hi love, its only me, I just needed to call you, we have got a letter from Bob's solicitors today and he has left us everything he had" I stuttered.

Silence, and then he said "I don't know what to say, what do we do, oh god, I am absolutely gob smacked. I'll have to have a think about it, I mean digest it all and then we can decide what to do when I get home, or do you want me to come home tomorrow?"

I explained there isn't anything we can do, this was his last wishes and it would happen whether we liked it or not and we just had to decide what we were going to do with it. Do we invest more in the business? We didn't want a new house. To be fair there wasn't really anything we wanted or needed.

Like with the funeral, we were in a privileged position, so we had just paid for it, never gave it a second thought, it's just what you do, but now this, well this was a stupid amount of money.

We decided eventually to both have a think over the next few days and we would sit and discuss it when Carl got home later that week.

As I came back in the living room my Mum and Dad said why not give some money to a dog's charity, Bob loved dogs and maybe the stroke society??

All good ideas but a couple of quid here and there wasn't going to make a massive difference. I had to get home to be alone now and think.

I laid in bed thinking, I would like to put some in trust for Louisa and James Junior, maybe enough for a car when they are older or a deposit on a house.

All the family could go on holiday.

We could expand the business even further and hopefully then Carl could take a bit more of a backseat.

We could pay off our mortgage.

We could give some to charity.

Oh, I really had no idea, we didn't need anything doing to the house, thanks to being married to a builder and all that Bob had done. We had the nice holidays, in fact we were very fortunate to have everything we ever wanted, apart from one thing.

A Baby, I know it hadn't been that long, but I was worrying that maybe we couldn't have children. I think I will go get tested, or maybe leave it and just see what happens, oh I don't know!

You dream of having money, having real money and I haven't even got it yet and I was stressing about it.

I might see if I could buy shares in the company I work for, as an investment.

We could even buy a couple of little houses and rent them out, again as an investment.

Oh Christ!!! I need Carl, sleep and a baby and no amount of money was bringing me any of that any time soon!

God knows what time I fell asleep but when I woke up I felt dreadful, I felt like I had only had about 5 minutes.

The rest of the week passed without any more letters arriving and I had just got back into my old routine when I realised Carl was due back that night.

I couldn't be bothered cooking and we had nothing in as I had forgotten to go shopping so I was going to suggest going out for tea.

As I got home I was surprised to see Carl's van in the drive, he was early.

I went in and he greeted me with his usual big kiss.

I found the letter and let him read it.

"Fuck me" was his reply when he finished.

"Right before we start talking about this let's have a walk up to the Outside Inn and get a pizza and have a couple of drinks.

The Outside Inn was a lovely restaurant. So called, because when you were inside, it looked like you were sat outside.

There were shop fronts and house fronts and even stars, it was fantastic for a pizza and always busy.

We went downstairs into the bar area, to wait until a table was available and discussed the letter.

I told Carl what I was thinking, and he agreed, especially about expanding the business, he had big ideas with what he wanted to do and the first was to build houses, from scratch.

He said it would probably mean setting up another company, but he had it all in hand.

I felt this wasn't just something he had plucked out of thin air, I think this had been an idea for quite a while and it was confirmed when he mentioned a plot of land he had seen in Rawdon that would be ideal for at least 12 luxury houses.

So, I think that was about settled, we would pay off our mortgage, leave some in trust for the kids and start a new building business, whilst keeping on the other, leave some to a dog charity and the stroke association.

We couldn't do anything until we saw the solicitor so that was the next job, get it all sorted, get the house sold and get cracking with our plans.

I had a feeling the business side was taking priority, Carl had definitely had these plans for a while and this had been the perfect excuse for him to mention it.

Chapter 33

I realised it had been a while since I spoke to Steve and I felt awful but then thought, well phones do work two ways, but I called him anyway. He wasn't in, so I left a message

"Now then stranger, have you forgotten who I am because I am not sure if I remember you, haaaaa, can you give me a call if you fancy a pizza and a pint anytime soon, byeeee." I hung up, hoping he wouldn't leave it too long to call back.

By the time I got home I noticed my answer machine was flashing.

"Now then even stranger stranger, only me, I would love a pizza and at least four pints so call me back, byeeeeeee to you too" came the message from Steve.

I called him straight back. We laughed about our various messages left and decided to meet the following night, at the Outside Inn, 6 o'clock and last one buys the drinks!

If I go to that place anymore I would start getting a staff discount.

I knew Steve would be early, he always was so I guessed I would be buying, I hadn't told him anything about Bob's Will, for all we were now good friends, I didn't really think it was anyone else's business.

I walked down the stairs, down to the bar and yes, he was there grinning like a smug southerner who wouldn't be buying any drinks!!!

"I did get you a drink in though" Steve said whilst pointing to my drink on the table.

We had a really good catch up and talked about Bob again, keeping his memory alive and then we talked about Steve's job, he was loving it and doing really well. I think he will make a fantastic nurse.

We covered just about everything possible and left to walk through the park, we both loved the park, it had become a regular place for us and for Steve it was his little bit of heaven, where he rented was just a room, no garden, nothing, so he came here as much as he could.

He stayed in his rented house, for all it was a bit grim, because he was saving to buy one, once he had qualified and when he had worked out what area he would like to live in.

I secretly thought he wasn't without a bob or two and he certainly wasn't living on a trainee nurses wage, he may have inherited a bit when his Mum passed away, who knows and who cares really, it wasn't anything to do with me.

We sat for ages talking in the park and he was reluctant to come back to my house, he was maybe tired, I didn't take it personally.

We said our goodbyes and arranged to meet soon and not leave it as long next time.

I watched him walk away and I found myself looking at his bum! he was a fine figure of a man, I hadn't really noticed before and I really shouldn't be looking but as they say "Look but don't touch"

I was lost in my own thoughts on the short walk home and next thing I knew I could hear the phone ringing through my front door.

I managed to get to it before it rang off – "Clare? Its Dave, can you come straight over, I think Jane is in labour and I have no idea what to do and her Mum isn't answering her phone" said Dave, very flustered.

"I would but I'll have to get a taxi as I have been drinking but I think you might be best calling the hospital, time her contractions and ring the hospital, they will ask how far they are apart and if her waters have broken" I said.

"That's the thing, I don't know any of this, you are so clever and to say you haven't ever been pregnant never mind had a baby" said Dave.

Alright mate don't go on, I thought.

"Dave, stop twittering, get Jane to tell you every time she is having a contraction, write the time down and wait for the next and then write that time down and keep doing it and that will tell you how far apart they are, or you could time in between each one. Whatever is easiest for you but keep a note of them and ring the labour ward, they will tell you exactly what to do and then let me know what is happening.

There is no point me coming over but if you need anything ring me." I said quite sharply really but I didn't need him reminding me I hadn't been pregnant yet, don't I bloody know it and I couldn't be arsed with Jane telling me how difficult it was and how fucking brave she is and how amazing it all was.

Yes, I was jealous, and I didn't give a shit and with that I went to the kitchen and opened a bottle of wine. I left it to breath on the side whilst I climbed up to the top cupboard again for my secret stash of B&H.

The wine had been breathing for at least 40 seconds, so that was ready.

I carried the wine, a glass and the B&H and lighter into the garden and sat on the step and enjoyed both. Just as I was sat there Mr Archer from next door came out to water his plants.

"Hello, my lovely, ooh you look like you are having fun" said Mr A.

"I am thank you, would you care to join me for a quick glass of red" I asked whilst showing him the wine.

He did a little look over his shoulder and nodded and started coming over "ohh that would be lovely, I am partial to a little red" said Mr A.

I went inside and got him a glass and we sat quite happy chatting away, drinking the wine. After about 10 minute he thanked me for my lovely company and the lovely wine and said he had better go water his plants.

It was beginning to be a bit of a habit, me drinking alcohol with various men during the week. Well if my husband is to work away what is a girl to do!

The wine was finished but I fancied another fag, so I went in and made a quick coffee, you can't beat a fag and a coffee. I sat, quite content and then the pissing phone rang again. I knew exactly who this would be.

"They are every five minutes and her waters haven't broken but she is in soooooooooo much pain" said Dave.

"Oh, hi Dave" I said sarcastically "If I were you, I would take her down, they might be able to give her something for the pain, ooh sorry love someone is at the door, I will speak to you later" and I put the phone down.

He had already said I had never been pregnant or had a baby so why the fuck does he think it's ok to call me? Stick your pregnant wife up your arse Dave!

With that I took myself to bed, not before I unplugged the phone. Call me pathetic or selfish but I didn't care, THEY were pregnant, so THEY could give birth, and they could go Fuck themselves.

Serves me right really because at 4.50am the following morning my phone rang. How I hear you say, because someone, naming no names, forgot to unplug the upstairs phone as well as the downstairs one, can't think who would be so stupid!!!!

Anyway, so the phone rang and woke me up, it was Dave, to tell me THEY had had a baby, a boy, no name, how Jane was amazing, and he was so proud (sticks fingers in throat) and that they wanted to make sure we found out from them and no one else. I didn't quite get that, and I don't think I would have been that bothered, particularly not the mood I was in at the moment when it came to them two.

"That is fantastic news Dave, I am so pleased for you all and I will ring Carl straight away and tell him, he's home tonight, all being well, so we will pop down to the hospital if that is ok" I said in my best gushing voice.

I put the phone down to the proud Dad and thought I would leave it for a couple of hours to ring Carl. I don't think he will be that bothered anyway.

I was right, he was pleased for them, but I don't think he would have been as pleased if I had woken him up to tell him. He didn't think we should go down to the hospital tonight, but I insisted.

It gave me a good excuse to go shopping, I called into GAP, they always had cute boy's clothes. Then I went to Thornton's to get the obligatory box of choccies for the proud parents.

Carl and I met outside the hospital, I hadn't seen him in nearly a week and it was weird seeing him in public, I could hardly stick my tongue down his throat in front of all these people now could I.

I loved him being home (even if I did quite enjoy my single life) the comfort of having someone around was lovely.

We went to see the new happy family and I have to say for a new born he looked quite cute, Jane looked knackered but then she had for the last 9 months so I don't know why I was so surprised.

She had to stay in for a couple of days as she had torn, it took me a minute or two to realise what she meant and once I did, my fanny actually contorted, bloody hell its worse than you think but totally worth it when you look at what you get at the end of it.

Carl had a cuddle and he looked so lovely holding him, like that Athena poster, only he wasn't naked.

I think Carl was a bit jealous though as he hardly spoke to either of them and wasn't really that interested in the baby.

One day I thought, when it is meant to be.

We stayed for ages and Jane explained the parents had been earlier on and how pleased and proud they were.

Once Dave opened his mouth to tell us how amazing it was and how he had so much admiration for Jane and that he had felt every contraction with her, I gave Carl "The Look" which basically said, "get me the fuck out of here NOW" and he got it.

"Right well, we will see you when you get home and we are so proud of you both, but the parking is going to run out" Blah Blah blah.

Carl was pretty good at reading me. We gave all three of them a kiss and promised to be over once they were home.

Once we got home it was still quite warm out, so we sat on the patio and opened a bottle of wine (it's beginning to be a bit of a habit) just as we were sat, Mr A appeared and said "Oh, have I been made redundant" I laughed and winked at him – Carl looked very confused.

"Private joke babe" I said and laughed.

"Come and join us" said Carl, but Mr A thanked us and refused saying he didn't want to intrude and he would be back to his post once Carl went away again.

He was so cute and very funny.

We had a lovely night and it got to about 10 when we realised we hadn't eaten so we ended up with toast for tea but neither of us were bothered, we were back together and that was all that mattered.

We fell into bed that night, happy to be back together.

Chapter 34

We got a phone call a few days later to say Jane and the baby were home and did we want to call round for a takeaway (Jane couldn't possibly cook, she had just had a baby and Dave couldn't as he too had just had a baby)

Great what a way to spend the last night with Carl, round there! I was being awful, and I had to stop it, but I was very jealous, and I had to really try hard to not be so nasty. If I wasn't pregnant after these few last days I don't know when I would be.

We had a nice night, nearly like old times, we had a laugh, not too much to drink and a nice takeaway and the baby was so good, he was perfect, but the poor little bugger still didn't have a name. Isn't there a law that you must register them within so many days??? The way they were going he would always be known as baby.

Dave explained because they had had such a tough pregnancy from start to finish they hadn't had time to think of a name!

We went through a few ideas, I thought Billy or George, Carl said Carl and they said they still had no idea.

Carl was at it again, not really joining in, then it hit me, he was really suffering with the fact we hadn't been able to have a baby as I still wasn't pregnant, oh bless him.

Things were getting more back to normal after Bob dying.

Carl and I were back into a routine and we both seemed to be coping. I was happy catching up with Jane and Dave and Steve and my Mum and Dad and Lilly, now that she had two children she spent more and more time at my Mums, moral support and a bit of help I think, so we made a point of all meeting up at least once a week for tea at my Mums with the kids, my sister, Mum and Dad and my Grandma, it was lovely.

I think I was due another night out with Steve, I would have to call him, but I was so busy at work I never seemed to get around to it.

I was sat at home one night, I'd been working late so decided I would have a night on my own when the phone rang "Get your kettle on" said Steve and the phone went dead.

Next thing there was a knock at the door.

"Coffee, one sugar please" said Steve stood on the doorstep with a grin on his face.

"What are you like you tit, showing off because you've got a mobile, well don't think I will be calling you on that, it'll cost a fortune" I said and welcomed him in.

We sat in the dining room drinking coffee and eating biscuits and he said he had been in the park and thought he would call on the off chance.

I loved it. I loved people just calling in and I wasn't one of these that wanted people to make an appointment to come and see me. I would always make any caller feel welcome at my home and Steve was no exception. I could chill on my own at any time, in fact, he actually made my night.

He hadn't been inside my house before, so I took great pleasure in showing him round, he loved it and quite honestly, you couldn't not love it, it was perfect.

He said he had been looking at a house down at the bottom of Horsforth on Newlaithes Road, it needed a lot of work doing to it, but it was a bargain. I said I would get Carl to look at it with him to give him an idea what costs he was looking at.

It would be lovely to have him so near, it was only a five-minute walk and it was something he could get stuck into, getting it just as he wanted.

He had quite a lonely life, work hours were not the best for making and meeting friends, not when you were at home when most people were working or vice versa, he did have a few friends, but he didn't ever really mention them or any wild nights he had been on.

Carl quite liked him but to be fair Carl only quite liked anyone, apart from me obviously.

Well I thought Steve was lovely and I just wished he could find someone that would make him happy, as happy as I was.

My Mum and Dad took to him straight away and welcomed him in, to be fair they welcomed anyone in, I think that's probably where I get it from.

Even Lilly liked him which was a rarity, she didn't like anyone, I don't think she was that fond of herself either.

In fact, I thought next time I go to Mums I will invite Steve, I think he misses the family side of things and I am sure he will adore Louisa and James Jnr.

It was tomorrow that I was meant to be at my Mums so no better time than the present to invite him, he was delighted, and I wished I had done it sooner.

"That's a date then" I said, and Steve smirked.

I picked him up the following tea time at his house and we drove to my Mums. As we got there we could hear all the noise coming from the garden.

"I'm guessing there are more people here than just your Mum and Dad" said Steve.

"Well I hope it's not my Mum shouting chase me, chase me" I laughed, and Steve joined in.

We were still laughing when we walked into the garden.

My Mum came running over, gave Steve the biggest hug and proceeded to talk to him in her poshest of voices and very loudly, as if he were deaf or foreign. Bless her she never got it quite right.

We played with the kids and Scamp in the garden when Steve noticed the Wendy House.

Steve loved seeing Scamp again and thought it was great that he had settled in so well and the bond between Scamp and my Dad was lovely,

"Is that your forever house" he enquired.

"Yes, fantastic isn't it, Carl and Bob made it for us, it is my perfect, forever home only I would quite like mine built out of brick and slate and to be a little bigger" I said.

"It's fantastic, I bet the kids will love it and it will bring so many memories to them when they get older, I love things like that" he said.

We had tea and then Mum brought out her piece de resistance, a carrot cake, it was delicious. Mum was turning into the proper Fanny Craddock.

We waved Lilly and the kids off, joy of being a parent is you must leave early, and we enjoyed an hour or so, just chatting to my Mum and Dad.

Both Steve and I really enjoyed it. He was very grateful to have been invited and to be included into our family.

I actually felt sorry for him, he had no family, miles away from where he grew up and a handful of friends. We need to get that changed I thought and I went through all the eligible girls at work that might do but they were all either too young, too old or too fucking ugly. He deserved someone special as he was a very special person.

Isn't it funny how you can just click with someone straight away, it's almost like Bob planned it.

I still thought about Bob a lot and missed him so much, having Scamp at my Mum and Dads helped as that was part of him and Mike from work kept calling in, now that he knew where we lived, even that was nice as he kept Bob alive with his stories.

Well that was another day over and another nearer to my man coming home for a few days.

I spoke to Carl before I went to bed and he said he had some news for me.

He sounded cheerful, so It wasn't bad news I was sure.

But then, you never know do you.

Why did I always worry and twitter about things and not just live in the moment.

Worry about it when you need to worry.

Chapter 35

I didn't have long to wait to find out because when I got home from work the following night he was home. It was a lovely surprise and he had made my tea, even if I didn't really feel like eating as soon as I got in.

"So, come on then, what's your news" I enquired.

Carl explained that he had had the offer on the plot of land accepted and that he was getting a team of men together to start building in the next few months or even weeks.

The plans for the luxury houses had been accepted, so it was just a case of getting the right men for the job, advertise them and Bob's your uncle, Fanny's your aunt, so to speak.

I was a bit annoyed if I am honest. We hadn't done anything with Bob's house, that was to all sort out and sell and I thought the business, was our business, that we made decisions together, especially since the money he was using was our inheritance from Bob.

I just felt I should have been asked about it and would have had time to think about it.

Too late for that obviously.

"Can I at least look at the plans and the plot of land" I enquired.

"I'll take you up after tea and the plans are in my van" came Carls reply.

After tea he drove us up to Rawdon, there it was in the middle of nowhere, a mass of derelict land.

There was an access road, so that was something and it seemed to go on forever.

"So how much of this have you bought" I asked.

Basically, he said the main field was ours, but you had to buy a bit more at the side, that wasn't worth anything as it was covered by trees and no one would want to use that.

Again, that was that. We drove home and when we got in I asked again to see the plans. They were good, nice big detached houses with all the latest mod cons.

The current building company were going to build them.

Again, Carl had decided he might as well use the current name as it was a trusted name in the world of builders, I wasn't asked about this either, but hey ho.

As we sat going through everything, the phone rang, Carl answered, it was Dave and Jane inviting us to a naming ceremony for Baby.

Carl wasn't impressed, the miserable git, he really didn't seem to like Jane and Dave at the moment.

Hallelujah, at last the baby had a name. I wonder why they are not getting him christened? We still didn't know the name of baby, we had to wait nearly two weeks to find out at the naming ceremony.

I was beginning to get that feeling again, Carl had thrown himself into this new project without any input from me, not pleased, we had to go to a naming ceremony for a baby with no name, great, and Carl wouldn't have noticed if I had danced round the house naked with a brush up my arse all the time he was home. I couldn't wait for him to go.

Fuck my life yet again!

And I still wasn't fucking pregnant!

Work was even shit, well it wasn't it was my mood that was shit and the only thing to do when your mood is shit is shop, so I did at lunchtime. I went to Debenhams to see what they had on offer to make me feel better.

They didn't have anything that took my fancy, but I managed to buy a vase for the house and as I was paying I looked over at an important looking lady behind the counter with the cashier, it was Lisa, I used to go to school with her. I hadn't seen her in years. It was great to see her, we chatted for ages and we arranged to meet up. She was still in touch with quite a few from school so she was going to get in touch with them and we would all meet up.

Well that lifted my mood and maybe when I meet them one of them might be perfect for Steve. Ooh bring on the reunion, this was all going perfectly.

Lisa rang when I got home that night, she hadn't wasted any time and we arranged a meeting at Fat Franco's on New Road Side a week on Thursday.

Sorted, I was going out, on a work night, with girlfriends and I couldn't wait.

The next day flew by and before I knew it Carl was back, and we were spending the weekend sorting the last few things of Bob's from his house, so we could get the decorators in and get it on the market.

It's funny but when someone dies, something in their house dies too, the house was cold and uninviting now, not at all like when Bob lived in it.

You could walk into Bob's with all the cares of the world on your shoulders and as you left they had gone.

It was one of those houses that you always felt safe in and comfortable but that had all gone. It was just a shell now and I couldn't wait to see the back of it. It wasn't Bob's anymore, but it would make a wonderful family home for someone.

We went for the fourth time to the tip and back to Bob's house. It was empty now and the decorators would be in on Monday.

I had planned for the estate agents to come the following week and get it up on the market. I don't think there would be a problem selling it, it was a perfect size in a perfect location for a family.

We were shattered by the time we got home and just chilled in front of the TV saving our strength for the naming ceremony tomorrow.

I couldn't wait to find out what Baby was going to be called but more importantly than that I knew that once that was out of the way it was only a few days to the reunion from School. I decided I wasn't going to tell Jane just yet, I would but just not yet. Anyway, she wasn't going out as she was a mother! Mother fucking earth if you ask me.

Chapter 36

The day of the naming ceremony had arrived, today was the day "Baby" got a name.

We arrived at Janes and Dave's at 2pm as requested. Both sets of parents were there, my parents and Grandma were there and a few other people that I didn't know.

We were handed a drink as we arrived and were all just chatting and milling about when an announcement was made.

It was time for the naming ceremony.

We all gathered round, and a hush descended as Jane entered the room with "Baby" in her arms, dressed in the most hideous sailor suit I have ever seen, the poor little bugger. This was all for show and very dramatic.

Dave then asked us all to take a seat, to which Carl shouted, "where to" and laughed.

Dave didn't find it funny, in fact neither Dave nor Jane seemed to find much funny these days, now they were parents.

Dave carried on and read:

"I would like to thank you all for coming today to help myself and my wife celebrate the birth of our gorgeous, happy and healthy baby boy into this world.

As you know from when we first found out we were pregnant (I am saying nothing) right through to the final push, my wife, my soulmate, my hero, my baby Mummy (that was a new one) has been sooooo brave and soooooo patient and soooooo amazing coping with it all, I think it is only fair that we toast her first."

"Or her fanny" I whispered to Carl.

"I couldn't have got through this last 9 months without her" he continued.

No shit Carl, as she is the one with the fanny and was the one carrying the baby, not you, you plank.

"She has been amazing, and she is the best Mum anyone could ask for. She has the patience of a saint and the nurture of a mother."

"She is my rock; my son and I are extremely proud to call her Mummy" said Dave.

Bloody hell, just a few weeks old and he was already calling her Mummy, now that is clever, I thought.

Now wait a fucking minute Dave, for one, babies can't talk, two, please do not ever, ever and I repeat ever, call her Mummy.

She is not your Mummy, the same as you were NOT pregnant, I thought, and Carl knew exactly what I was thinking, I could tell by the smirk on his face.

Dave carried on. "It gives me great pleasure to advise you all that from today, my son and heir, oops, our son and heir, is to be known, as (drum roll and lots of tension building) Carlton"

Well, I didn't see that one coming. At least he had a name.

"Do you think Jane helped Dave with the speech" whispered my Grandma with a wink as she walked over to the buffet.

Carl and I couldn't contain our laughter when mother and father earth joined us.

"How amazing was that, it was such a surprise, I had no idea he was capable of writing something so moving and touching, did you?" said Jane.

"No, we had no idea he could write something like that either" said Carl trying not to laugh.

"I don't know if you have wondered why we aren't getting Carlton christened, but you see, we thought about it and felt that because it is only us two that could ever have created this perfect little man, that it was only right that we write and hold the ceremony in our family home, you see, we are a family now and family is everything" said Jane.

"Carlton can decide, when he older, which path he will take, and we will respect that, wont we Dave?" said Jane, in a mother earth tone.

What the fuck has happened to her, did she push her brain out at the same time as Carlton? That had made my mind up, I most certainly WOULD NOT be telling her about the reunion. She's a bloody freak. I get it, well I don't actually, that having a baby is the most wonderful thing in the world but come on, she is not acting like a normal human being, she's always been a bit quirky, but this, this just takes the piss, and she had been a bit off with Carl but to be fair he had been a twat and hadn't bothered with any of them.

We had a couple of more drinks, there wasn't a lot as Jane is breastfeeding and they said that.

"Drinks are limited people, obviously due to breast feeding" said Dave.

"I didn't know I had to do it too" laughed Carl and so did everyone else apart from Jane and Dave. Carl had been partaking in the beer a little too long and his tongue had got very loose.

Yup, she definitely had pushed her brain and humour out at the same time as pushing out Carlton.

"Right well we had better get off, thank you for including us in this special day for Carlton" I said, and it was quite sad as it was so staged, it wasn't how I have ever felt around Jane or Dave, but things change, people change, and I had to accept that, we were growing up and apart and I wasn't sure I liked it.

Carl and I walked home and spent half of the walk doubled up in two, re-enacting the speeches and how the two of them talk now. In fact, at one point, we were half way through the park and I had to stop to try catch my breath as I was laughing that much, and Carl wasn't helping at all as he kept on.

As I looked up I saw Steve sat on a bench, "Steve" I shouted, and he looked up. Carl and I walked over to him, still laughing.

"How are you doing?" Carl asked as I couldn't speak for laughing.

"Yes, good thanks, I'm just waiting for a friend" said Steve.

"Oh right, well we won't keep you" said Carl and turned and nudged me to follow.

"See you later, have a good time" I said before I started laughing again.

I wonder who he was meeting, I thought as I looked back to see if I could see anyone.

Nothing? strange I thought. Steve was soon pushed out of my mind as Carl started again with his impression.

We were still laughing when we got home.

I just couldn't believe that two people could change so much in such a short time and we had no idea why.

My sister had 2 children and she wasn't a bit like that.

Well she was odd, she had always been odd but not odd in a Jane kind of odd, if you get the drift.

Odd, that's all I can say, they are very odd.

Chapter 37

Well it was time to say goodbye to Carl again, ooh too soon. My life was back on track, we had had a lovely day and he had promised me I could go book a holiday this week, so everything was looking good.

Monday, Tuesday went by without much happening but by Wednesday lunchtime I thought I cannot wait until the weekend to book a holiday, so I went in my lunch hour, to book New York, Vegas and Hawaii.

Well we could afford it, why not.

I couldn't wait to tell Carl but first I had to plan what I was going to wear to the reunion, after all I hadn't seen these girls in years, I had to make sure I looked amazing.

I rang Carl as soon as I got in to tell him all about where we were going, a few days sightseeing in New York, Vegas would be a blast and a chill and relaxing time in Hawaii.

It wasn't for another few months, in fact it was ages away, but he seemed excited and so was I, plus it gave me something to talk about at the reunion.

Talking about the reunion, that must be one of the funniest nights I have had in a long time.

I got there about 10 minutes early, thinking I could get a drink, sit at the bar and I was then in prime position to watch them all come in.

I ordered my drink and went to get my place when I noticed someone was sitting where I had pictured I would sit, as I walked over she turned around.

It was only one of my old school friends, Tracey, I hadn't seen her since we left school, but we had been best friends at Primary school.

I said, "trust you to be sat in prime position, I was going to do exactly the same."

"Great minds think alike my friend, how are you" said Tracey and we hugged.

We talked and talked, in fact so much so that two other girls had walked in and we hadn't noticed, they obviously didn't recognise us or maybe they felt threatened by our beauty.

Lisa arrived, late, and she kind of gathered us all up, which is when we noticed the two others.

I wasn't bothered about seeing most of the others, but it was fantastic to see Tracey and Lisa again. We all sat down and the three of us managed to get sat together.

We went through the usual:

	Clare	Tracey	Lisa
Married	Yes	Divorced	Married 2nd time
Children	No	Yes, Two	Yes, Three
Job	Manager	Teacher	Retail Manger

They couldn't believe I didn't have children, but like I said, it just hasn't happened yet. We decided we had all done well for ourselves considering the things we got up to at school.

We remembered going up to a shop at lunchtime just up from school, it was run by two lovely ladies and they used to let us go in the back room and we would buy toasties and smoke fags and drink coffee. Perfect.

We would also knock off school on a Wednesday afternoon as it was double PE and it really wasn't our thing and who needs PE anyway, we all got B+ marks on our school reports, so that just shows you how much the teachers noticed.

We would go into town on a Friday night to the Bank and Panama Joes and get the night bus home. The bus home was sometimes the highlight of the night.

Before we knew it, the others were putting their money on the table and making their excuses to leave.

I wouldn't mind but I had never heard of one of the women, she looked tons older than us and I certainly didn't recognise her, I think she was an intruder.

We three carried on drinking and laughing until we were chucked out at closing time. Lisa got picked up by her husband and Tracey and I walked home together as we realised we only lived a street apart, yet we had never bumped into each other, but then we do tend to drive most places, so we wouldn't would we.

She came in for a coffee as my house was the nearest. As we walked in she was amazed at the size of it, it was a bit of a Tardis and she loved the kitchen.

As I was making the coffee she noticed the plans to My Forever House.

"This is unusual, is this a house your husband built" asked Tracey.

I had mentioned he was a builder. "No, it's one I designed, it's my dream forever house and I told her the story of how Carl built it as a dolls house for me and how he used that to propose.

I then pointed over to where the doll's house was.

"Oh god that is amazing, how lovely to go to all that to ask you to marry him, that is so romantic. I love it and it's an amazing house, you have very good taste but then I know that because you are a friend of mine" laughed Tracey.

We sat talking for ages, but we still had so much to catch up on.

"I am going to have to go or I will never get up for work, look I'll give Lisa a call and we will arrange to go out again" said Tracey.

"I tell you what, arrange to come around here when Carl's away and I can cook us something" I said.

So that was arranged, we exchanged phone numbers and said we looked forward to catching up again soon.

I went to bed that night exhausted but so happy that I had rekindled a relationship with one of my oldest friends.

I laid in bed thinking about all the things we used to get up to. God we were buggers but we had a right laugh.

Happy memories, and with that I fell asleep.

Chapter 38

So, the decorators had finished at Bob's and the house was on the market and we had just accepted an offer.

End of an era but onwards and upwards.

Carl was home and we had planned spending time alone just pottering about and not doing very much.

When he got in that night I noticed he went straight upstairs. He did that every time he came in and it took me ages to work out what he was doing.

I remembered he did it one night when I was going to bed so I looked round the room to see what it could be, then I spotted it, the safe.

I walked over and opened it, fuck me! I had never seen as much money in my life, there was thousands and thousands.

Now I knew builders had their little dodgy deals (not all builders obviously) but I thought that was what Carl was putting in a bank account in my name. That already had shit loads in and now this. All I could think is I hope we never get burgled, they would have a field day!

I couldn't be bothered asking him about it, he would just say it's nothing, don't worry, it was a Bobism that he had picked up.

We decided to have a trip over to my Grandmas, I went most weeks and saw her at my Mums, but Carl didn't get much chance to go over now, with him working away so much, and he loved it at my Grandmas, she was always baking, and her house had that homely safe feel.

As we got there, Grandma was just getting some scones out of the oven, she looked really pleased to see us and gave us both a big kiss and a hug and put the kettle on and then said "You could smell those scones couldn't you Carl" she laughed.

"Ohh go on then if you twist my arm" said Carl whilst giving her a squeeze.

She loved it and set about making the tea and getting Carl his scones.

We chatted for a while and my Grandma brought up the naming ceremony again, she said she had never been to anything so strange in all her life.

Coming from my Grandma that was massive as she never said anything bad about anyone, ever.

After our tea and scones we decided to go to Harry Ramsdens, we hadn't had fish and chips for ages, but I said we could go only if we could eat them outside.

We used to do it as kids, go to Aireborough swimming baths for lessons and then sometimes up to Harry Ramsdens and if we were really lucky we could go in the fun fair at the back.

We got there, and they were queuing, they always were, it was a popular haunt. We eventually got served and sat on one of the wooden tables. They were bloody lovely, the fish and chips, not the tables.

All that was missing was a cup of tea and a ginger biscuit, you can't beat that after fish and chips.

Well we had had a lovely day and now we were back home and again we sat in the garden, Mr A was out, I am sure he waits for us.

"Before you say no, I am going to insist you come and have a little drop of wine, take it as a thank you for looking after my wife while I am away" said Carl to Mr A.

"Well if you put it like that, I can't really refuse can I" and again he looked over his shoulder, to check for his wife I think, before he came over.

You didn't see much of his wife, she had had a stroke a few years ago and didn't come out much, she just sat in the front room, near the window or sometimes in the back garden but not very often.

Mr A regaled us with tales of when he was headmaster at a school in Otley, it sounded very strict, but he loved it, yet he also said he loved being retired.

He was quite sad when he said he and his wife only had a short time to enjoy retirement before she became ill. He was always saying to us to enjoy life to the full while you can, drink the wine, dance in the rain and sing with the birds.

That was one of Mr A's favourite sayings.

Well it was getting dark; the wine was finished, and I was shattered.

We all said goodnight and headed off.

Once inside Carl mentioned the houses again.

They were starting to build them next week!

Oh, just throw that one in there Carlos, it's not like it's a massive project and a massive risk or anything.

He went to his van and took out all the literature he had had printed.

"They do look amazing, but I thought I was helping to choose the interiors "I enquired.

"I know love, but I gave it to one of the girls at the office to do, you have enough on your plate" he said.

Oh yes like being stuck on my own 5 days a week is really having enough on my plate, I was looking forward to choosing everything but never mind, yet again I had been left out of the equation.

We went to bed and I was sulking, so Carl changed the subject to our holidays, he knew just how to get me back on side!

Time was going so quickly, before we knew where we were we were signing the paperwork for the estate agent and completing the sale on Bob's house.

All done and onto a new chapter.

Tracey had rung me a few days after our last meeting and her and Lisa were coming around tonight.

I had prepared pate and French stick and a lasagne, made from scratch, well not the lasagne sheets but the béchamel sauce and the mince filling!

I didn't bother with a pudding as I knew we would be drinking and I can't do sweet things with alcohol, unless I am forced.

Food ready, white wine chilling, red wine breathing, music on, a collection from the 80's obviously, you can't beat Adam and the Ants, Kajagoogoo, Mel and Kim and Rick Astley ooh and not forgetting Culture Club.

They were both bang on time, they had bumped into each other on the drive.

Both stood waving two bottles each as I opened the door.

This was going to be messy!!!!

As soon as they walked in Lisa wanted the grand tour! That was Lisa to a tee.

As we finished I poured us some drinks and we clinked our classes and cheered each other.

I was in the kitchen when Lisa said, "I love that drawing on your wall, is it one of the new ones your husband is building" Asked Lisa.

I explained It wasn't but told her all about it, how I designed it as my dream house and how he had them drawn up properly and she laughed as she turned around and saw the Dolls House. That's so sweet, Aaaah I get it now!

"So, you drew the house, Carl did it properly, then he made it into a doll's house and proposed to you, so now all is left is for him to build it properly when you start a family and live happily ever after" said Lisa.

"I can't wait to meet him, does he have any single mates, I'm ready for husband number 3 – we all screamed with laughing.

"Forget you, I would quite like number 2 if I can" said Tracey.

We had another drink and then I thought it was time we started the first course.

We chatted all the way through that course and the next.

It was like we were all 15 again. I only saw a few from school and so did the others really. You soon lose touch as everyone has busy lives but meeting back up with these two, I knew I wouldn't lose touch again, we don't have to live in each other's pockets, but we will always be there for each other.

The question of what had happened to Jane came up, so I explained we were still in touch and the four of us were still friends but how she had changed since she had given birth, they both had and it's almost like now they are parents and we aren't they can't be friends with us anymore.

That was just how I felt. It wasn't for the want of trying, believe me, but it hadn't happened yet.

Both girls listened, and I think I was going on a bit and Lisa just said, "Well she's always been a bit odd let's be honest" and we all howled with laughter.

Another bottle of wine was opened, and we retired to the living room.

"Get some tunes on Clare" said Tracey as she spotted the HI Fi system.

"I might have a few 80's tunes in there ladies if you are interested" I said showing them our vast collection of all things 80's, after all it was our era and we still loved the music now.

Mel and Kim's "Respectable" belted out, we were all up dancing and laughing.

"Do you remember when we all bought those big hats thinking we were Mel and Kim" said Lisa.

"Oh god and do you remember we would wear suits and swap jackets, like Mel and Kim did" said Tracey.

"The best ever was a night at Ritzys Tracey do you remember, half way through the night we swapped clothes, completely, we went to the loo and swapped and when we came out no one noticed" I said, nearly crying with laughter now.

"No, the best was that night we bought a bottle of duo tan, you, me, Lisa and Jane and we covered ourselves head to toe and we all woke up that night sweating and we panicked we had put too much on and we were going to die" said Tracey.

"Oh god yes and your Mum went mad because it was all over the sheets in the morning "I said, "and we didn't wash our hands, so we were orange all over including our hands."

We laughed again remembering, that was hilarious, we had all decided we wanted a tan and Duo tan promised to give us sun kissed skin, sun kissed my arse, it looked like we had been tangoed. We all tried to shower it off, but we looked like Umpah Loompas for about a week and no amount of makeup covered it. Happy days though.

We were shattered now with all the dancing so we all sat down and had another drink.

We then got around to naming people we had been to school with and wondering what had happened to them.

Most of our old school friends had moved out of Horsforth, a few to places far away but majority round and about but it was amazing you didn't see them, but would we recognise them, we were all getting older. Ok so we all looked the same, but I am sure some didn't.

Before we knew it, it was past midnight and we were all getting too old for late nights. We promised to meet up soon and said our goodbyes.

I tidied up and went to bed thinking of life back in the 80's, the carefree days of worrying about who fancied who, where we were going that weekend and what the best shade of lipstick was! Happy days.

Why do we all take things for granted, we never stop and look at what we have, we had no cares or worries really but you don't appreciate it at the time.

It's the same with anything, you never appreciate what you have till it's gone.

Chapter 39

Carl had rung earlier that day to say he wouldn't be able to get back that night as he was snowed under and he would try to get back the day after.

This was becoming a regular occurrence and to be honest it was really upsetting me, he loved his work and he was passionate about this new project, but it was taking over his life, our life, but it wasn't for ever and we did have our massive holiday to look forward to.

I rang Tracey when I put the phone down to Carl to see if I could call round for a coffee, silly question, of course I could, I was welcome anytime and so was she at mine.

I walked round and was greeted by one of Tracy's daughters, she was so cute. She was called Emily and she was five and a half, as she told me when she opened the door.

"My Mummy is in the other room putting the kekkle on for her friend, are you her friend?" asked Emily.

"Can I be your friend too" she asked.

"Erm yes I am Clare, your Mummy's friend and I would love to be your friend" I said to the little dot in front of me.

With that Emily took my hand, led me to the kitchen where Tracey was and announced, "Mummy this is my friend Clare, say hello".

Emily sat with us for a while before saying she was tired and taking herself to bed, Tracey went up after 5 minutes and settled her in and checked she was ok.

Back downstairs we just chatted about general things and the latest goings on in East Enders and Coronation Street, we were both massive soap fans, I guess that's all you had when you were alone during the week.

It was lovely having Tracey so near and then it came to me, Steve, oh my god they would be amazing together, so I told her all about him.

She agreed he sounded nice and said she might be up for a drink, but could I invite him to mine and she would just call in, just passing.

That was sorted, I would call him tomorrow and make arrangements, but I wasn't allowed to tell him about her, it had to be an impromptu visit!

I started thinking about all the things the four of us could do. I loved being back in touch with Tracey, then it hit me. I had done the self-same things years before, with Jane, when we planned what the four of us would do and look how that had ended.

It got me thinking about them more and I was saddened at how things had turned out, but we had nothing in common anymore. Carl couldn't be bothered with them, out of jealousy I think as they had a baby and he didn't, and they couldn't be bothered with us.

It was sad.

Next day, when I got home from work I was straight on the phone to Steve inviting him round the following Wednesday. He was delighted with the invite and said he would be with me at sixish.

I phoned Tracey and told her the plans. She was looking forward to it too.

Just call me little Miss Cupid!!!

This was going to be excellent, I could feel it in my water.

A couple of hours later the phone rang, it was Lisa.

"Hey love, just thought I would give you a call, you ok?" said Lisa.

We talked for about ten minutes and then she said:

"Have you got something to tell me? I know I haven't seen you for a few weeks, but I thought you would have told me."

I had no idea what she was talking about.

"So there I was walking the dog when I thought I would go down to have a look at the houses Carl is building, they are looking fab by the way, anyway, the dog spotted something and ran off, busy chasing him I didn't realise I had gone to the back of the houses when I saw it, your bloody House, I know I said Carl was sweet for doing the plan and the doll's house and the Wendy house but to actually build the fucking house, Oh my god does that mean you are pregnant? Oh shit, no more boozy nights for you for a while. Mate, that is amazing! Why didn't you tell me? Oh god was it a surprise, weren't you going to say anything to anyone till you moved in, well your secret is safe with me, I won't mention it again, but I am so pleased for you, don't worry Mums the word." said Lisa, not pausing for breath.

She quickly changed the subject but continued to talk to me for about another 5 minutes, then I heard one of her kids shouting in the background and she said she had to go, she would speak soon and hung up.

I sat with the phone to my ear until the awful buzzing sound started and it jolted me into reality and I put it down.

What was she on about? My House? Carl had built it? Was it a surprise? Oh God, was it? And she thought I was pregnant, if only!

Then reality hit me, shit, that was why he was working away so much, he was building me my house, I guess the other houses must be selling well.

I cannot let him know I know and when it all comes out I will tell Lisa to never let on.

Oh god this was amazing, I had to go look, was it too late now? Nah, I'd get over there now, but I would have to be careful he didn't spot my car. When he took me that first time there was a plot of land behind the houses, I remember him saying it was nothing and they wouldn't use it. Like you would buy land and not use it, it was all clicking into place, there was only one thing to do now.

"Tracey, it's me, I need a massive favour, are you and the girls up for a little drive out?"

So, we were off, me and Tracey and both her girls in the back, excited at going out for a drive. By the time we got to Rawdon the girls had fallen asleep, I directed her to the site and I could see on the drive up how much they had done on the other houses, they were all up and looked like they were nearly finished.

We parked up and I couldn't see anyone about, no vans or cars so I pointed over to where the other bit of land was, neither of us speaking as we got nearer, my heart was racing and as her lights caught the clearing, it lit up the house, my house, my forever house my dream house.

We just stared at each other, there was no mistaking it, it was my house.

We sat there for a while and then headed home, in silence.

We got back to Tracy's and I helped her carry the girls up to bed and as we got back into the kitchen Tracey poured us both a glass of wine.

"Well it looks like I might be losing my favourite neighbour" said Tracey.

The reality of it all hadn't sunk in, after all I had only known a couple of hours, how was I going to keep this to myself? I had to, I couldn't spoil this now, Carl would be devastated so I had to pretend it hadn't happened and I was just glad Carl wasn't at home, at least only seeing him every few days was easier, and it wouldn't be forever.

The house looked finished, I would have to start listening to him more, he will start hinting soon surely.

I thanked Tracey for her help and left to go home. Yet again, that night I didn't get much sleep, I was too busy designing the interior and wondering if it would be exactly the same as I had initially planned, it certainly looked it from the outside.

He really was amazing and full of surprises, even after all this time!

How weird but if I hadn't bumped into Lisa at Debenhams that day, I wouldn't have met her, and she wouldn't have known about the house, fate, that's what it is.

Carl was home the next day, he didn't mention or hint at anything and I was conscious not to let him know I knew so I kept the topic of houses strictly off limits, we had a lovely couple of days and then it was back to reality.

Tonight, was the night, Steve was coming around so yet again another little white lie. I made his favourite, spaghetti bolognaise and garlic bread and waited for him to arrive, which he did at six, on the dot!

We chatted and had our food then at about seven, the door went, surprise surprise it was Tracey.

"Hi love, how are you, come in" I said in an over loud voice.

"Sorry to bother you but the girls are at their Dads and I was at a bit of a loose end" said Tracey in an equally loud voice.

Tracey came to join us, I introduced them to each other and Tracey gave me the "mmmmm" look. I couldn't tell what Steve was thinking but he was his usual charming self.

To my horror after about an hour Steve excused himself saying he had an early shift in the morning and he said his goodbyes and left.

Not quite how I thought it would go but at least they had met.

Tracey was impressed, and I promised her I would call him in the next couple of days and see what he thought.

Well it hadn't gone exactly to plan, I thought Steve would have stayed longer but I guess if he was working early then that can't be helped.

He was chatty enough and was quite charming, in fact very charming.

I was sure they were going to hit it off, to the point I had worked out what all four of us would do together.

Chapter 40

The weeks were flying by and still no hint or sign from Carl, there was only one thing to do. I would have to have a closer look, look inside and see how far off it was from being finished.

Carl was down in London, so I knew he wouldn't be at the house and it was after finishing time, so I knew none of the builders would be there.

I drove over and was surprised to see that the other houses were now completed and most of them sold so the barriers had gone, and it was easy to get in. I parked my car near my house and walked up the path.

I looked in and couldn't believe what I saw, it was all ready, freshly plastered walls and by the look of it they had been painted too, as I walked round the outside of the property all the rooms were the same.

All ready for me just to decide a colour scheme. I knew wall paper was out of the question for a month or two as the plaster had to settle and I was quite liking the freshness and cleanliness of all magnolia. It looked new and clean.

As I walked through to the back garden, I just stood and stared, I couldn't believe my eyes, there at the back of the freshly lawned garden was "My house" a replica, just like the one Carl had built for my Mum's garden, only this one would be for our children, in our garden, at our forever home.

I was so happy I could have burst with pride. Who would ever do such a thing, he was fantastic beyond belief and It took all my willpower not to ring him and tell him how much I loved him.

Who could I tell, I needed to share this with someone and get their opinion, was I imagining it.

I walked back to the car and just sat there, was I imagining it all, was I looking for something wonderful and convinced myself this was it.

I looked at the proof, when Carl and I first came to the site he dismissed that plot of land, the house was my house, the one I had designed, no two ways about it and there was a replica in the garden.

No, I was not imagining it, this was going to be the biggest thing anyone had ever done for me and there was only one person I could tell. One person that was removed enough from us not to let on to Carl yet was close enough to be able to share this with and them be pleased for us.

As I got home I picked the phone up straight away and dialled.

"Steve, it's me, are you busy?"

Half an hour later, I was back at the site, plan of my house in hand and stood in front of the new build, I passed the drawing to Steve and said, "look at this then look over there, what do you see?

"Wooooah, it's your house" exclaimed Steve.

Just the confirmation I needed.

"When did this happen, when are you moving?" Asked Steve.

I explained how I had stumbled across it, thanks to Lisa and how I was doubting myself that Carl would do something so fantastic but that he (Steve) had just confirmed exactly what I was thinking.

"Well that certainly beats anything I could ever do" said Steve.

He didn't look that impressed, in fact he seemed quite miffed.

Rude, I thought, this was one of the biggest things to happen in life and he didn't seem the slightest bit interested, in fact he seemed quite bored now, so I subtly suggested we get back home and I dropped him off.

I couldn't believe one minute I was on top of the world and now thanks to Steve I felt a bit miffed and cheated somehow. Well he can go shite, I thought, no one is going to spoil this for us. Screw you Steve and screw your bad mood!

I was meeting Jane the next day and it again took all my willpower not to tell her, once upon a time we told each other everything but since she had become a mother we had grown apart, but I was sure we would get back to where we were once I was a mother too.

We did the usual, cooed over the baby and asked each other how we were and what we were up to. I told her I had bumped into Lisa and Tracey but didn't tell her what a fantastic few nights out we had had, it wouldn't be fair, she wasn't going out, now she was a mother.

When I got back home Carls van was on the drive, my stomach lurched, oh god this could be it, this could be when he tells me, after all it was all finished, there was no reason for him not to tell me.

I walked in and we greeted each other as we usually did when we had been apart for a while and sat down to have a coffee. Nothing, nil, zero, zilch, he never mentioned the house, even when I quizzed him about the other new builds, he just said they were now all sold and onwards and upwards to some more new builds.

That is why he had been in London, he was branching out and building down there, the money was stupid, and this was the one that was going to put the company name on the map.

Well that was that then, it wasn't going to be anytime soon now was it.

The next few days were quite strained between Carl and I, I think mainly because I knew this whopping secret and I didn't want to spoil it for him, I was actually glad to wave him off a few days later so I didn't have to keep up the pretence.

Driving home from work that night, I couldn't help it, I found myself at the house again only this time there was a van outside, one of the builders, so I had to be very careful that they didn't see me. As soon as I spotted the van I did a quick 14-point turn and got out of there but as I was driving away I looked over and saw something that made me wince a little, Carl was there? He was meant to be away.

Driving home I couldn't get this out of my head and then decided he must be putting the finishing touches to the house under the guise that he was away. Of course !!!! haaaaa how stupid am I, well I can play along with that, the little superstar that my husband was.

I rang him when I got in and he confirmed what I was thinking, he was working away and really busy. Yeah right Mr, you have to get up earlier than that to kid a kidder!

I left it a few days until Carl was back home when I decided I would pay another visit to my house, knowing it must now all be finished as Carl was home.

Driving down the lane to the house I was singing away to myself feeling on top of the world. I drove very slowly as I approached just to make sure no one was there. No vans, but there was a car parked in front of the house and I could see the front door was open. Oh god burglars I thought then realised there was nothing in the house so what were they going to pinch!

I parked way back near the other houses and could just see enough through the trees, I would use the story that I had bought one of these houses and was just looking at it again if anyone questioned why I was there.

I sat for ages until eventually someone came out, a woman, about my age, I had no idea who she was, maybe an interior designer. Well there was only one way to find out.

I got out of the car and walked over, deciding I would stick to the previous story and I approached her.

"Hi, sorry to bother you, I have just come over to look at my house, I've bought one over there and saw you, so I thought I would come and say hello as it looks like we are going to be neighbours" I lied. Secretly laughing on the inside.

This is the part she tells me she is doing an undercover job for the builder for his wife as a surprise as she designed this house and he has built it for their forever home. Feeling very smug!

"Oh, you made me jump" she said as she turned around clutching her very pregnant stomach.

Oh, bless Carl he had given her this job, obviously one of her last ones before she has a baby, it would give her extra cash.

"I am actually just moving the last of my things in, I'm due in two weeks but I don't think I will go that long and my partner was meant to get this ready before but there had been a lot of hold ups but luckily it's just ready to move in, come in, I will make you a drink, neighbour" she said.

"This is your house, what, baby due? moving in? you can't be, I don't get it? I mumbled and just kept going on and on, in complete shock and total confusion.

"Are you ok" asked pregnant lady, "You don't look very well" she said concerned.

I managed to pull myself together and apologised and said I had been under a lot of pressure at work and buying the house and just ignore me and yes, I would love a coffee.

Jesus this was going to take everything I had to find out exactly what was going on here without hitting her across the head with the new Le Cruet pans she had on the side in my fucking kitchen.

We sat chatting and it all came out, from her, don't worry I would be getting an Oscar for my performance.

She had started working for Carl ages ago, they had fallen in love, he was married but his wife died, funnily enough the same time Bob died, then she found out she was pregnant and well the rest is history.

He had designed this house years ago and when he bought the land it was perfect for this house, so the plans had been approved and then when she found out she was pregnant it all fell into place, perfect.

Fucking perfect all right, the lying fucking arsehole, wait till I see him, I will cut his fucking dick off and post it to the queen. The cheating, lying bastard!

I felt my world had come crashing in, tears were stinging my eyes, I couldn't quite take in what had just happened, what I had just found out. I had to get out of there, I was going to be sick and I couldn't use the excuse of spewing, all over her knew parquet flooring on stress.

I made my hasty excuse and left, running to the car I threw up and kept throwing up. I could see her looking over, I had to get out of there and fast.

The tears flowing now I sped out of the estate and onto the quiet lane.

I sat there, I screamed, I hit the steering wheel about forty times, screamed some more and cried, I cried and cried for what seemed like forever.

I had an ache in my heart, this was what heartbreak felt like and I cried some more.

Why? What had I done or more to the point what had I not done, given him a child. This was what is was all about, that and he couldn't keep his dick in his pants, the bastard!

Before I knew what was happening I found myself at Janes door and fell into her arms sobbing uncontrollably.

She and Dave managed to get me into the front room and sat me down. Jane sat and hugged me, rocking me like a baby, stroking my hair and hushing me.

We sat like this for quite a while and when I managed to control myself enough to talk it all came out. The affair, me dying, the house he designed and the woman and the child.

"What an absolute CUNT" spat Jane, totally disgusted. She had a way with words I will give her that.

We threw a few more obscenities into the frame.

What was I going to do, we couldn't move on from this, never, this was too much.

"You have to try and behave as normal as you can, I will ring him in an hour and say you and Jane have gone out and you will be staying here. You have to keep your calm, he will be away again in a bit and in the meantime, I will decide how you are going to leave him and with what you are entitled to" said Dave.

I was totally beside myself, my whole world had ended, it had all been a lie for over a year. How could someone be so cruel, have an affair ok I get that but to say I was dead and build her my fucking house, that was crazy, he was living a double life and you are not telling me no one at work knew.

I said as much to Dave, he dropped his head.

"What is it, what do you know" I screamed, I just knew there was more to this.

Over the next hour Dave explained how he had caught Carl out with the woman ages ago, the same time as we stopped being close to them. He had caught him and given him an ultimatum, stop seeing her or he will not have anything to do with us and how was Carl going to explain that one.

Easy I thought he just said they were weird and convinced me I didn't need them. What a twat! It was all making sense now.

"I am so sorry, but I thought he would come to his senses but deep down I knew this time would come and I have been ready for him and planning what to do for you, you deserve a good life with someone who is honest and trustworthy" said Dave.

This was all very well and good but how the hell was I going to stop myself from killing him.

Dave did as he said and told Carl I was sleeping at theirs, not that he would give a shit, he would be straight round to hers now, oh sorry MY FUCKING HOUSE, that she was living in.

Well to say the next few weeks were hard was an understatement they were horrendous. Carl had no idea I knew, how the hell I did it I have no idea, but I did, I wanted him to pay and know just how much he had hurt me and by keeping calm it would all happen.

I had transferred all the money out of my bank accounts to a new one as I knew Carl had all the details. Dave must have been hatching this plan for a long time as he had thought of every little detail.

All I wanted was enough money to get a house, the real money or the business didn't interest me, all it had brought me was misery and I couldn't give a shit about it, been there, done that and it was fucking shit, so a nice little house would be perfect.

I was earning a decent wage and really didn't want thousands in the bank, it was more trouble than it was worth. It had changed Carl completely and I was hoping it hadn't changed me.

The next step was a visit to the solicitors where I explained I wanted out, I wouldn't be asking for half of everything as I didn't want it, but I wanted a divorce on the grounds of adultery and unreasonable behaviour and anything else we could chuck in for good measure.

He would not be allowed to contact me, ring me, visit me or talk to me, it all had to be done through a solicitor which was one good thing.

He would receive the papers once I was gone.

I had explained everything to Daniel at work and he had been amazing, I sat there crying and snotting and he was brilliant and said to take time out and if I wanted I could move to London and work there for a while until things were settled but why should I move down there, I had done nothing wrong so I decided to take up his offer of a bit of time out and booked a holiday for me and Mum where I would explain everything to her.

Dave had sorted me with a flat to rent while I sorted everything out and I would be moving in tomorrow, once Carl had set off to work.

Carl, the lying, fucking, arseholey excuse for a husband.

Chapter 41

D Day- Carl had gone and literally as soon as he had, Jane and Dave appeared to help me get my things out and take them to my new apartment, just around the corner from them. It was nice and new, and it would be my haven until I found a house.

Jane and I packed all my clothes, what ornaments I wanted and photographs, Dave went to the loft to get the Christmas decks, (he really had thought of everything) and other bits and pieces I wanted.

I wanted a complete fresh start from Carl so most could stay, I just wanted my stuff.

We then emptied every safe in the house and Jesus there was a lot of money in them but as Carl said, no one knew it was there, certainly the tax man didn't and I was owed it.

All my bank accounts had been changed and I had enough for a house, so I was happy, that was all I wanted, a fresh start.

As we put the last of the things in the car I posted letters to my favourite neighbours explaining briefly what had happened and how I had moved on and that one day I would come back and see them.

We sat in the car ready to go, waiting for Jane, what was she doing? She eventually arrived, sat in the car, laughed and said, "Let's do this" said Jane, "don't look back, it's onwards and upwards now my love" she continued.

It was years later, I found out what Jane had done, she had put cress seeds on the carpets and watered them, knowing Carl wasn't home for a while and then put prawns in the hems of every curtains in the house and wacked up the heating on full!

I had to give it to her, that was fantastic!

All the stuff dropped at my new abode the only thing left to do now was to pick up my Mum and take her on holiday for two weeks of glorious sunshine in San Diego, California. She had relatives there and we would call in to see them, but the rest of the time would be talking and enjoying ourselves.

My Dad knew something wasn't right but knew I would tell him when I was ready. I thought if I told my Mum first she could break the news to my Dad.

No one knew any of this only me, Dave and my best friend in the whole wide world Jane. They had come up trumps and I was so grateful to them.

Chapter 42

We were staying at the Hyatt in San Diego, overlooking the harbour and I decided to give my Mum 24 hours peace before I dropped the bombshell.

"Mum, you know you asked me a while ago if everything was ok as you and Dad were worried about me" I said one afternoon as we were sat having a wine cooler in the roof top bar.

"Oh, dear god you are dying aren't you, I knew it, oh god my love, what is it, how long do you have" said my Mum.

"Mum! I am not dying, well part of me has died, I have left Carl" I said and waited for a response which took quite a while.

"Thank God for that, I mean that you aren't dying, why, what has happened?" she asked, looking concerned.

I explained his lying and cheating and how he had been living a double life, made me not have much to do with Jane and Dave as they knew he had a girlfriend, how he said I had died and how he was going to be a Dad and moved his happy family in to my dream home.

I also explained that until today he had no idea I knew, he would have received his solicitors letter to my old house, his work address and the address of my Forever house. I am guessing by now he will be a Dad and I hope he has the balls to own up to this woman or it will happen again I am sure.

He can't contact me or any of my family unless they contact him first, which I stressed I am hoping they won't as even them contacting him to shout and scream at him would give him the opening to talk to them and try find out where I am, if he was that bothered.

My Mum bless her, sat and listened, tears streaming from her eyes, she let me get it all out, the hurt and the confusion, the meeting with the other woman, finding the house in the first place and how elated I was that he had built it.

Once I had finished I cried and she sat and hugged me then went to the bar and ordered a magnum of champagne and passed it round to other guests sat in the bar and stood up and said, "Here is to the bright and amazing future of my amazing and brave daughter" and the bar erupted

They had no idea what was going on, but the yanks love a pissed up, frightfully posh middle aged mad woman making a complete spectacle of herself and so did I, god bless my Mum, she is hilarious.

Jane called that night and said Carl had been round to theirs and was banging on the door asking where I was, he had obviously got the letter. Dave had apparently walked outside, smiled and then punched him and told him in no uncertain terms to "Fuck right off, you piece of absolute scum, go back to your double life and crawl back under the stone you came from, oh and I hope you can sleep on a night knowing you have broken the one good thing you had in this world, Clare, she is worth a thousand of you now fuck off before I hit you again and do not ever come here again or try contact my family" he watched him walk down the path, his head bowed and then Dave shouted again "I am sure Bob will be really proud of what you have done"

They watched Carl as he sat in his van, head in hands, reality had got him! Karma was a bitch!

I wasn't happy, but I was glad he knew and hopefully once me and Mum were home we could start and put things back together.

The rest of the holiday was lovely, very relaxing and just what I needed.

Before we knew it, it was time to say goodbye to California and hello England and my new life.

Chapter 43

Work kept me very busy and I am guessing Daniel had told my close friends at work what had happened, I am sure he didn't go into full details, but they were all lovely on my return and before I knew it, I was back and loving life again. Well, I was whilst I was at work, but I am not going to lie I was still spending most of my evenings crying and feeling very sorry for myself.

It was going to take time and I knew that but when you have been with someone for so long and grown up with someone it is hard to cope, it's almost like a death. That person has died and that was the only way I could cope with it, dealing with it in that way.

The prospect of house hunting was daunting but I knew if I was to fully move on then I had to get out there and do it so that is just what I did.

Jane and I spent hours looking at various houses, I had enough money for a decent house, but I wanted to stay in Horsforth and it didn't look like my money would stretch that far. That was until we came across a beautiful old Victorian house, down at the bottom of Horsforth. It had been empty years and needed a lot of work doing on it.

I decided to call Mike and ask if he could give me a rough idea of the price.

I had arranged to meet Mike the day after at the house and I had managed to blag the keys from the estate agents on the proviso it was only the builder that went in as they weren't sure how safe it was.

Mike was there when I got there with a big grin on his face, as I got nearer I saw he wasn't alone.

"Now then love, how are you"? he said "I have brought a couple of the lads, we have looked round the outside, let's have a look inside and I will see what needs doing"

About half an hour after they all came out with the "ooh this is not going to be cheap" look on their faces.

"Well, if this is the house you want then we can do it" said Mike.

"That's great but how much are we talking" I asked

"Don't you worry about that love, trust me" he turned to the lads to go and continued " I know what's gone on and I think that ex of yours is the biggest twat on this planet, to do that to you is fucking stupid so I'm going to tell him that we can do this for you, for nowt like, it's the least that bastard can give you" said Mike.

I didn't understand at all, but basically Mike has said he was calling all the lads off their latest site, he was telling Carl that materials and labour would be free and that once my house was complete they would all go back to work.

"He won't fall for that one" I said.

"Oh, he will, I know more about his dodgy dealings than anyone, one call to the VAT man and he's screwed, he has got off very lightly by doing this" he said

And that was that.

Oh god, I was about to have a second chance at my dream house and this was just that, a fresh start, still in Horsforth and it was a beautiful three storey Victorian house, lovely patio garden at the back and the only neighbours were two houses just up the lane. One with a retired woman living in it and the other a gay married couple that were thrilled at the prospect of finally having a new neighbour.

If we could pull this off it would be perfect.

So basically, Mike was blackmailing Carl for all the shitty things he had done to me.

Mike knew far too much about Carl and his dodgy dealings for him not to agree to it.

Like Mike said though, he is very stupid, is Carl, and should he say no that wouldn't stop the lads, they would do it anyway. Carl couldn't afford for them all to leave, it would ruin him so there was no way he would say no.

Mike was pulling the lads off their current jobs to get my house sorted.

Apparently, the lads were gutted when they had heard what Carl had done to me, they liked me and said I had always made time for them.

They were going to do everything I needed to get this house habitable, from new roof, new windows, new heating, new kitchens and bathrooms, re wiring, plastering and painting and a bit of TLC.

"It's a piece of piss" said Mike.

"It will only take us a fortnight and you will be moving in" said Mike sounding very pleased with himself.

I got the call I wanted the morning after "We will be with you in 3 weeks" said Mike "you had better get that house bought".

Luckily the purchase was simple, I didn't need any surveys doing as the builders were taking care of all that – I handed over all the money and within a week it was mine.

Just two weeks and the building would start.

Jane and Dave were so excited for me and so was Baby Carlton, he was growing by the second and every time I saw him he gave me the biggest smile that made everything else seem so insignificant.

Chapter 44

Because I had the house before the guys were due to start, a few of them came over a few times and planned a list of everything they would need. They even brought me brochures of kitchens and bathrooms for me to choose, it really was going to be all done and complete and ready to move into.

I had decided to have a separate little room at the front of the house, like Bob's sun room, just to sit and chill, then a dining room, a sitting room and the kitchen running the full length of the house. A staircase would take you up to the second floor where there were two bedrooms, both en-suite and a room to be used a gym (yeah right)

Top floor was my bedroom and en-suite with sky lights.

It would be perfect and all I had to do was chose the kitchen, three bathrooms and what colours I wanted.

Because the house had such big windows it was very light and airy, so I decided to keep the colours bright.

I also decided that I wouldn't buy any furniture until it was all done and then I could go and chose it all and get exactly what I wanted.

Jane and I loved this bit and each night we would go up and have a look.

All the outside still had scaffolding on for quite a while and we weren't allowed inside so really, I don't know why we bothered as there wasn't much to see but it was so exciting, and it gave me a purpose and something to look forward to.

It was nearing the end of the builders allotted time and we had seen them there very late at night a few times. They all worked so hard and were determined to finish it for me. Every time I went to check they were all ok they would tell me, with pride, what they had done. I owed them all so much, I just could never repay them.

Finally, the day had arrived to go see the finished house.

As Jane, Dave, Carlton and I pulled up outside the house there were about twenty builders all outside waving.

Oh my god I felt famous. We got out of the car and Mike met us.

"Are you ready love, I think you are going to love it" said Mike.

He led me into the house and it was fantastic, better than I had ever imagined, he had managed to restore a lot of the traditional features but introduced modern ones too.

It was so light and beautiful; the kitchen was to die for and it had a built in bloody coffee machine. At the back of the house were steps down to a secluded patio garden that they had filled with pots of flowers, it looked amazing.

Upstairs the two spare rooms and en-suites were like something out of a boutique hotel and my bedroom was so luxurious it was out of this world and it had a dressing room and a walk-in wardrobe.

Mike then pointed to the Hollywood Mirror he had made for me, you know the mirrors with bulbs all round them.

"That is for you, you are our star and a very special lady, don't you ever forget that" said Mike and with that he planted a little kiss on my cheek.

We went back outside, and I thanked each one of them for all their hard work and told them to all be here next week for a party.

I now needed help buying new furniture as I had nothing and with my Mum and Dad and Grandmas help I was able to afford better than I had budgeted for.

Everything was falling into place and this time next week I would be in.

When everyone had gone I went back with Jane and Dave and thanked them for everything they had done for me and that I really couldn't have managed without them, they had been amazing, and they were the best friends I had ever had and ever would have.

As I left I decided I wouldn't go back to the flat but back to My House, my new home.

I just wanted to have another look, take it all in, on my own and relish every second. I had the chance of a fresh start and I decided life is too short and that I was going to grab this chance by the bollocks and have the best life I could.

As I opened the door, it was so peaceful, but it felt so right.

I walked over to the kitchen, touching the freshly painted and newly plastered walls as I went.

I was just in the kitchen, admiring my new, state of the art, built in and better than the mothers, coffee machine when there was a knock at the door.

"Whoo Hoo, Only Us Darling, Bruce and Sid at the rescue"

As I went over, it indeed was, my new neighbours, holding a bottle of fizz.

"Just thought we would bring this as we saw you come in, to welcome you home" said Bruce.

How lovely I thought, these two were fantastic and I just knew that we would have some right parties once I had moved in properly and I couldn't wait to get to know them better.

Sid produced three glasses and we did just that, we toasted new beginnings and the start of something wonderful for me and my new forever home.

Chapter 45

The party was a great success, all the builders and their wives and partners came, my family, Jane, Dave and Carlton and of course my new neighbours.

The lady (Mary) was away but Bruce and Sid were there, they were full of it and had everyone in hysterics.

I got a load of meat and beer and wine and did a Bar B Q and we played music and laughed and the wives all said what a bastard Carl was, and we laughed and for the first time in a long time I realised I could laugh about it.

Yeah, I seemed to have wasted a lot of my life with a man that was leading a double life but up to the point of his indiscretion we had had some amazing times and I did love him and he made me what I am today. He gave me the love I needed at the time and the encouragement to do what I wanted and now somehow, he had given me the courage to go to the next chapter in my life and that is what I was doing now.

As I waved them all off I poured myself a large glass of red and I went outside and sat on the back step, looking at my beautiful garden with not a hint of any dolls houses in sight and I thought this is it Clare, you have survived. Part of me would always love Carl as he was the love of my life and like I said we had some amazing times but now was the first page of my new book.

I was daydreaming when I heard a knock at the front door.

Someone must have forgotten something I thought, and I went to open it.

"Steve" I said, I haven't seen you in ages, come in, how did you find me" and just as I said that he hugged me, and it wasn't in his usual friendly way but a way I hadn't felt in a long time.

Then he pulled back, took me in his arms and kissed me and I have to say it was bloody amazing.

I have no idea how he found me, but I had a pretty good reason why he found me, and I wasn't going to complain.

He always knew what to do and when to do it, maybe, just maybe the first page of my new book was going to be something of a romcom!

Also, I thought I had found it then lost it, but I think I now have my forever house.

Isn't life just bloody great.

ABOUT THE AUTHOR

Born in Horsforth, Leeds.
I am not a writer, I am just a working Mum and wife with a dream to write a book, so I hope you enjoyed it.
Never say never, dreams can come true.

28189040R00157

Printed in Poland
by Amazon Fulfillment
Poland Sp. z o.o., Wrocław